Really Odd!

Gilly Wilkinson

For Jean & Mike

The sequel!

Lotsa love

Gilly

x

BARKERS PUBLISHING

First Published 2007

ISBN 978 0 9554543 1 8

A royalty of 50p is given to EACH for every copy sold

Published by

BARKERS PUBLISHING

7 Station Road Trading Estate, Attleborough,

Norfolk NR17 2NP

Printed by

Barkers Print and Design Ltd.

For Florran and all her friends.

My thanks go to Serena, Sue & Peter,
Angie & Mike, Nathan, Jennie, Ruth,
Jay & Steve, Colin, Dave, Elizabeth,
The 'We Care' appeal,
to everybody who helped with the preparation of this book
and to you for buying it.

Written and illustrated
by Gilly Wilkinson

Really Odd!

Chapter One

The sun was streaming in through the cottage kitchen window where Peanut sat at the table mesmerised by a huge red egg. The red backed buckle bums egg! The year was almost over and any week now this egg was due to hatch.

Large and shiny in the sunlight, the egg sat snugly in a viewspaper and cotton nest. As Peanut watched, it was rocking slowly to and fro, to and fro. It was quite hypnotic. Then, every now and again it shook violently, almost impatiently. Peanut was entranced. "I wonder what a hatchling looks like?" she thought excitedly. She had never seen anything like this and had no idea of what to expect.

Boris had tried to describe the poor gangly featherless hatchling that was likely to emerge, but Peanut hadn't even seen a newly hatched chicken or skylark so it was difficult to imagine. The chance of anything hatching in the house of Peanut's parents had been minimal and therefore not something that Peanut had thought much about, let alone witnessed. Just then Bean appeared from the garden and stood in the open doorway.

"Hey Peanut, come and help us with our swing," he grinned cheerily. "We put it in the huge oak tree so its bound to swing right up to the moon." He danced impatiently from one foot to the other while he waited for her to join him.

"Great, only I hope it doesn't REALLY go up to the moon. I think I've have had more than enough excitement for a while, don't you?" she asked peering up at him. "Do you think the egg will hatch today? Only, I don't want to miss it."

"Are there any cracks showing on it yet then?" he asked curiously, regarding the egg with interest.

"No, it is still intact, although it does seem to be a little more active today," she added as the egg jumped almost a full centimetre off the nest. The viewspaper in the nest wafted gently in the sudden air current.

"Come on, it will be okay. You'll miss all the fun if you don't hurry." Bean tugged at her sleeve. "Pa Baddle had to climb almost to the top of that oak, it's the one near the gate. That means the ropes on our new swing are the longest ever. I'll bet you have never seen one that will go as high as this one will."

Peanut took one last look at the rocking red egg and ran to join her friends. It was one of those excellent Friendsdays when you can hear the birds sing and laughter rings out all around. The sun warms your skin all the way through to your bones and you feel lazily content and at peace with the world.

Everybody greeted Peanut as she appeared. "Grief, look at that!" She was really impressed when she saw the new swing. Bean hadn't been exaggerating, it really was attached to the very highest possible branch. She grinned at Pa Baddle in admiration for his daring. Poppy was already in the seat of the new 'attraction' at the cottage, waiting for the maiden voyage over the garden wall and into the sky.

Lots of their friends were visiting today. They were sat on cushions and chairs scattered around the front garden, chatting, laughing and picking at the most amazing picnic ever held in the history of Odd. The food was so delicious that, despite already being so full that their tummies were fit to burst, the children and adults alike kept going back for 'just one more'.

The wish biscuits seemed to be going particularly well. Not because anybody needed a wish here in Odd, but more because it could taste of whatever your own favourite happened to be. So if you liked raspberry jam flavour, it would taste of raspberry jam!

Bean and Peanut had spent the previous evening having great fun, planning all the best things ever created for today that you could possibly manage at a picnic. Boris, Ma and Pa Baddle, their three children, Mrs Batty, Boots, Sandra with her new foster brother Jeremy from 'The World', and many varied craminals were all there. They were telling jokes, catching up on news and lazing in the beautiful sunshine.

Bean went to help by pushing the swing to get it started. He pulled the seated Poppy back and shouted, "Hold on", as he let the swing go.

Poppy whizzed through the air, hair streaming out behind her. "Wheeeeeeee!" she shouted as she sailed toward the wall. Then "Aaaaaargh" as she realised she wasn't going to clear it. She lifted her legs as high as she could to avoid the oncoming obstacle.

Sadly, the base of the seat caught the stones on the top of the wall and Poppy flew gracefully through the air, hair still streaming, but minus the swing. Her facial expression had altered somewhat too! Then came the inevitable 'CRUNCH' and Poppy came to a sudden halt (of the 'sore backside' variety).

Bean cleared the wall in one jump in his concern. "Poppy, Poppy, are you alright?" He crouched beside the quietly shaking girl.

"Owwwww!" she moaned.

But when he saw her face, Bean was relieved to find that she was actually shaking with laughter. As soon as he realised Poppy was okay, he started to laugh too. Pa Baddle was already halfway up the tree to shorten the ropes so there could be no more accidents.

Back in the kitchen, huge cracks had begun to show on the shiny red egg. It rocked then shook, rocked then positively bounced. More cracks rippled through the shininess like rivers creeping through a map.

Bean took his go on the swing next, just to ensure it was, "quite safe for everybody else," he assured them all, eyes twinkling. "Wouldn't want there to be any accidents would we?" he asked Poppy, with a serious face.

"Ha ha!" Poppy responded, thumping him cheerily on the arm. "No, that would be a shame wouldn't it?" she bantered.

It was while the children (and some of the adults) took it in turns to test the swings suitability for safety, and while the sun shone dreamily into the garden... while the adults (and some of the children) were chatting merrily through the afternoon, that back in the kitchen, with one almighty shove, a hole appeared in one end of the battered less-shiny egg. A tiny blue-grey claw-like hand snaked around the edge. Then another crept over the other side.

"RRrrr!" growled a tiny voice as the gnarled scratchy hands literally tore the remaining shell into two halves. One half was flung with such violence that it smashed to smithereens as it hit the floor.

There in the centre of the wreckage on the table, lay a defenceless bright pink featherless bird. Huge black eyes blinked sweetly in bewilderment. Beside it, in the same nest stood a tiny, ugly blue-grey man. His face looked as though somebody had cruelly pinched his cheeks between finger and thumb, then pulled.

Covered in a blue-grey fuzz, he was frowning and scratching his armpit. He drew back his fist and angrily punched the other half of the shell up into the air and off the table edge. "RRRrrr!" he growled. His eyebrows were going up and down as he turned around, taking in his new surroundings.

Everything in this room was tidy, except the egg shell of course. The chairs looked comfy and the floor looked clean. This room made him feel sick. He shook his spindly hairy legs, then walked to the table edge where he peered over, frowning.

Flexing his hairy claw-hands, he grasped the tabletop and swung himself over the side where he dangled momentarily and then dropped with apparent ease to the floor. He stood for a while behind the table leg, listening to ensure that the room was devoid of a witness. As soon as he could see that the coast was definitely clear, he ran to the door and was gone.

A few moments later Peanut, Bean and Poppy all entered the cottage kitchen for some lemonade. "Look!" exclaimed Bean, nodding toward the table. Peanut raced over.

"Oh, isn't it sweet," she stated, staring at the little pink bird. "Ahhh, It's gorgeous, look, it's blinking at me. Do you think I might pick him up? Would he mind?"

"I'll go and get Boris," Bean said, and he dashed back out through the open doorway.

Poppy said, "This is the first one I have ever seen hatched too. It looks as if hatching has been pretty traumatic, just look at the mess." She waved her arm back, indicating the shell particles strewn across the table and floor, all the way to the door.

Boris came dashing in with Bean. "So, you've hatched have you my beauty?" Boris enquired in hushed tones. The pink featherless mass blinked sweetly up at him with liquid black eyes. "Go ahead little one," he added to Peanut. "You can pick him up. I expect he will probably be glad of the comfort. He isn't nearly as delicate as he looks."

Peanut scooped the bird up into her carefully cupped hands. She cradled the tiny fluffy body in the crook of her arm. "Will his feathers grow soon Boris?" she asked. The red backed buckle bum opened his beak and let out the most beautifully haunting song. As he closed his beak at the end, he stared up at Peanut and blinked in total adoration. Her heart seemed to skip a beat as she gazed in amazement that anything could make such a lovely sound.

"You will need to feed him some grit and seeds mixed with water. There's no problem with you holding him because, as of today, you are his mummy. The red backed buckle bum gave the egg to you to take care of. It is a complete and utter honour for anybody to be bestowed. You will find your new offspring to be wonderful company and they are also meant to be quite magical. You'll see," Boris confided. He continued, "Each of these birds are different, just as any baby would be different to the next, although they all have a lot in common with each other too. We will not entirely know about this one, until he shows you what he is made of."

Peanut continued to cradle the fluffy fledgling. "My word," Boris added looking up. "I do believe it is raining. Well I never! How odd." He frowned, his glasses raised on the bridge of his nose. The children had never seen Boris frown before and it was a strange sight.

Sure enough, there on the panes of glass were droplets of rain!

Chapter Two

Out in the garden, the picnic began to get wet! The food had almost gone anyway, so from that point of view it didn't matter too much. The first reaction to the rain was that it went almost completely silent. Everybody stopped talking and stopped what they were doing. They simply stared up at the sky in total disbelief. They got quite wet doing it too.

Ma and Pa Baddle collected together some of the chairs and blankets, then made a move toward the cottage kitchen. Slowly others followed suit and started to gather belongings. Eventually everything had been brought in, out of the rain. Still they stared silently up at the sky, shaking their heads, puzzled. Rain didn't happen in Odd during the day, it was a simple fact. What on earth (or on Odd) could be happening?

At the local trap-stop, (similar to our bus stops only you were assured of a courteous and comfortable ride, free of charge and as and when you needed it!), three of the cottage guests had gathered for a ride home. Pa Baddle had elected to go on ahead with Henry, in order to light a fire in the hearth and warm their home through. Mrs Batty and Boot the dog stood chatting alongside them.

“I don’t think I have ever seen rain during the day in Odd,” Pa Baddle said, stroking his beard thoughtfully. “It is decidedly odd.”

“That is because it has NEVER rained in Odd during the day. You know as well as I do that it rains at night, of course it does. It’s NOT Odd, nothing like Odd in fact.” Mrs Batty rambled, shaking her head. They fell back into silence again.

Henry couldn’t recall daytime rain but he was only seven. He trusted grown-ups to know what they were talking about though.

Boots looked up to the sky and shook himself. His wet coat was beginning to smell and he was SO particular with his personal hygiene. He felt more than a little annoyed. Looking down into a slowly growing puddle, he suddenly stopped breathing. There in the puddle was a copy of ‘Zap the Wizard and the Land of Odd’. There were chunks quite literally bitten out of it! He shivered.

Just then, along the lane came the rumble and clip clopping of a horse and cart. It grew louder as the horse neared them. Boots looked up at a cloud, then down at the bitten book. He took a deep breath. Then, before he could stop himself, he said in his growly deep voice; “HOW ODD!” Then.....Whooosh! They all vanished.

The cart drew to a halt at the cart stop. The horse looked around expectantly, but there was nobody there. He put his head down and began to nibble the grass while he waited patiently for some passengers.

Boris swept up the eggshell. His friends and family sat around chatting about their day and admiring the new arrival. Peanut sat proudly, gently stroking her beautiful new baby bird. It seemed to Boris that it was only he who could feel a sense of unease. Something wasn't right. While he couldn't quite put is finger on it, he knew something was dreadfully amiss.

He looked around again. It wasn't just the rain pattering against the windows, although he would admit that, in itself, was unusual. There was a strange feeling in the air. He shook his head and took some tea over to the table. Things couldn't be all that bad, he tried to reassure himself. After all, here he was with all the people he loved and cared about. He should be counting his blessing, he nodded grimly.

Outside, a tiny tired blue-grey man yawned and stretched. He climbed into a tree hollow, curled up and fell fast asleep. Growling gently in between loud and furious snores. It stopped raining.

Inside the cottage, a sleepy pink bird sang his beautiful song to a room full of enchanted listeners, then he closed his eyes in gentle slumber. The sun came back out.

Eventually, Ma Baddle decided it was time for her and the boys to go home. "Pa will be wondering what has happened to us," she laughed. She kissed her young hosts on the cheek, kissed Boris, thanking them all profusely, then walked through the wet grass and puddles to the cart stop where happily, a cart was already waiting for her.

Strangely enough, the rain had stopped just as the pink bird had begun to sing, Ma Baddle mused as she jogged along with her boys in the cart. The grass glistened with rain and there was still a damp clingy feeling in the air, she noted. A most unusual state of affairs, she thought.

After a lovely tea, the rest of the guests began to leave, waving and chatting as they walked along the flower lined pathways to their homes. The air was heavily scented with a fresh clean earthy smell. Boris looked around him and shivered. Something just wasn't right. He went outside to lower the 'at home to visitors' flag and packed it away ready for next Friendsday.

......Pa Baddle stood shivering in the cold grey morning air, still stroking his beard, still with his companions, but there in front of him was a sign. One direction pointed to 'Fast Harling' and had a bright red heart on it. The other direction looked pretty plain and boring really. He clutched at his long black coat, pulling it around him for warmth. Along with his overcoat he was also wearing shorts and to complete his ensemble were his stout but old walking boots. He looked down at his boots for inspiration. His knees were all knobbly, looking almost embarrassed at being on such hairy white legs. He looked around him. Where were they?

Over in the nearby field, a blue tractor chugged and grumbled its way up a gentle incline where it was working, not alone, I hasten to add. The tractor was complete with driver. The entire area smelt strongly. Birds sang apologetically and cars roared. When a huge aeroplane thundered overhead, through the grey sky, they all threw themselves to the ground, terrified.

Next, a car hurtled past the strewn prone group. It screeched to a halt at the 'Give Way' sign as if it were paying homage to some kind of God, then screamed off again. Another aeroplane roared above them. Eventually, Pa Baddle got to his feet. He felt cold. His clothes, (apart from his coat) were only fit for a summers day. They were damp and not really fitting to a cold East Anglian autumnal morning.

Mrs Batty was helped to her feet by Henry and Boots. "What's Fast Harling?" she asked in a worried voice. Her white apron flapped around in the draught created by the speeding cars. In the distance the blue tractor chugged on.

"There there my dear Mrs Batty, you mustn't worry about a thing," Pa Baddle reassured her. "It can't be all that bad, look, there is a heart after the name. It must mean that this is a great place to be." he reasoned hopefully and not without logic.

Mrs Batty continued to frown and look worried. "Where are we?" she asked in a pitiful voice. "How did we get here? This is a most awful and unfortunate day", she finally declared, fiddling with her apron corner in agitation.

"Not necessarily my dear, there is always a reason for everything. Don't be upset", Boots soothed, "lets just sit here a while and see what happens".

"Good Idea", nodded Pa Baddle. "Somebody must be looking for us. Or perhaps our reason for being here will present itself, given a little time". He looked around him, "There is a great saying that goes 'when in doubt, do nowt!' He sat upon the verge and looked along the road. "This is an unusual style of crossroads", he remarked. "Look here, there are five ways of travel, not four".

They all looked politely.

......Back at the cottage, Boris was chatting with Peanut who sat contentedly, not wishing to disturb the red backed buckle bum. Bean had gone up to his room to listen to some music. Peanut could hardly believe that an entire year had passed since she had been handed the egg. It had been so much fun that the time had absolutely sped by. She was grateful that Poppy's arm had healed so nicely. They were all really great friends now too, she mused. "So, what are you going to name your baby then Peanut?" Boris asked, settling himself into the comfortable armchair opposite her.

"Sweetie is a really apt name," she grinned.

"Hardly," Boris laughed. "He is definitely a male and something tells me he would not be too enamoured with 'Sweetie' as his name!"

"Well, what about Andrea, because he has an enchanting voice? Or..." she paused, considering all the thousands of options. Then she discounted them because they simply couldn't do justice to the honour of such a magical and beautiful creature.

Boris stroked his chin thoughtfully. "Did you know that within a couple of weeks, this wonderful baby will be almost completely feathered. A month after that, he will be able to fly?"

"As quick as that?" Peanut felt a little cheated by this news as it meant that her care wouldn't be nearly so necessary and this saddened her. Her baby might just fly away and be gone! He wouldn't need her at all then.

"He will need to be able to fly in order to do all his good deeds. It is his birthright. I told you he's magical, but don't you worry", he nodded his assurance, "this little mite will still need you when he's fifty, let alone five. They are really loyal like that."

"Actually," he continued, "you are really lucky there. The females leave home forever after only a year in order to make homes of their own. They are nomadic and flit from home to home, as and when they choose. But, the males put down roots. They bond with you and they adore you forever." Boris smiled as he caught the look on Peanut's face.

"What about naming him 'Flame'?" Peanut asked. He will look just like one if he's as red as his mummy was, and he will have the power of a flame I imagine, since you say he is as magical as all that."

Boris nodded. "I like that," he agreed. And so it was that the red backed buckle bum was named. Flame stretched out his featherless fluffy wings and then snuggled closer in his sweet contented sleep.

......Somewhere in a tree hollow a nasty, growly, blue-grey man stretched and belched loudly in his sleep. A hunting owl swooped low, saw the grime-grazer and recoiled in horror. It couldn't be. A grime-grazer in Odd? He decided he was wrong.

Obviously he was just feeling overworked and overtired and it had got the better of him. It must have been a mouse or some other creature in a fancy dress costume that he had seen all curled up in the tree hollow. Grime-grazers hadn't been in Odd for hundreds of years. He must be wrong. All the same, he didn't feel like going anywhere near that tree again in order to check out his 'error'. He went home hungry.

Chapter Three

The next morning Peanut bounded out of bed. She padded across her bedroom carpet to the window and drew back the curtains. The weather was misty and she couldn't tell if it would be sunny after all. She was hoping to see Poppy today. They could chat about Flame and look up details of all the mystical things recorded about red backed buckle bums. They could play 'guess what Flame will be like when he is older' and plan the best way forward to care for him correctly.

Boris had loaned Peanut a book. She looked down at the sleeping bird and stroked his forehead. He was so warm and soft. Flame let out a contented sigh and opened his liquid black eyes. Blinking up at her, he opened his beak and sang. Peanut was moved to tears. "Flame you are enchanting and I love you so much. I am going to look after you and do my very best for you," she confided.

Flame carefully nudged her hand with the side of his head. She picked him up and carried him to the kitchen, where Bean and Boris were already eating a lovely breakfast of egg and bacon rolls. They were watching the rain dripping down the outside of the glass as they ate.

Suddenly the door flew open and in ran a red-cheeked, breathless Poppy. "Oh! Oh!" she gasped. Boris leapt to his feet. "Something awful has happened." Clutching her sides and leaning down on to the back of the chair for support, she lifted her head and said "It's Mrs Batty and Boots, they are vanished, GONE!"

"Sit down Poppy, ordered Boris looking at her ashen face. "Have a drink, and then tell us what you mean that they are gone. They can't just disappear, they have to be somewhere!"

Poppy drank obediently. "They are gone I tell you," she insisted. "They left here yesterday, before me. Don't you remember?"

Boris shook his head, trying to think back. "No, there was so much going on yesterday, what with the hatching and the rain."

"Well they did leave here before me," Poppy continued. "They were going to light the fire and warm the house all through for when I returned. But when I got back home, there wasn't even a light on. The fire hadn't been lit. I don't think they ever made it back home. I waited and I waited. All night, every sound, every creak and I sat up expecting them to walk in and say what a joke they had played on me, or what an adventure they had just had. But they never came." She stood up again, frowning and jumping from foot to foot, unsure of what to do next.

"It's obvious that you haven't slept Poppy. Just look at you, you are a bag of nerves and you are no good to anybody in that state, least of all yourself. Right, have that cup of tea and a bite to eat, even a little morsel will help and then go and have a lie down upstairs. You have done all you can and I shall take it from here,"

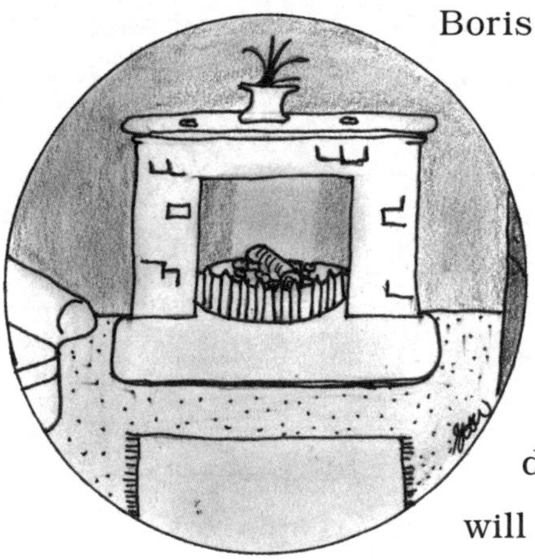

Boris assured her. Poppy nodded silently.

"By the time you wake I shall have located Mrs Batty and Boots and you will wonder what all the fuss was about. Perhaps they *have* had an adventure. You know how easily distracted Mrs Batty can be. Boots will have gone along with her to ensure no harm comes to her. He is a wonderfully loyal companion. You'll see."

Poppy nodded miserably. While she knew Mrs Batty wasn't like that and that despite her distractibility she always kept her word and followed all her little routines, she couldn't deny that she was tired and mighty glad that Boris was going to step in and help. She went to her room, next to Peanut's, fell onto the bed and into a deep slumber.

......The grime-grazer had woken with a growl. He scratched at his tummy with his gnarled pointy hand and stuck a finger into his belly button. Wiggling it around, he looked out into the sunny morning mist. Hungrily, he looked around him.

A butterfly flitted prettily by, once, twice, then a hand shot out and grabbed it. "Slurp, slurp, crunch, crunch." It was gone! The grime-grazer laughed and climbed out from the hollow tree and into the daylight. It started to drizzle. Next, his squinty eyes landed on a caterpillar. Grab! Holding the soft juicy body in his hairy hands he squidged it, dropped it and then wiped his hand on his hairy leg.

“Yuk! Too pretty around here”, he thought in disgust as he looked around. He ran from tree to tree in a stealth like manner. Hiding behind each trunk and taking a swift look around to assure anonymity, he made his way. Pausing every now and again to search out trouble, or worse, make it!

......After he had been awake for a minute or two the misty rain turned to huge droplets. Pa Baddle had waited and waited for ages. Apart from screeching cars, roaring aeroplanes and smelly fields, not a lot had happened. A weak sun began to cling to the grey sky in the cold morning air but it warmed nobody. He shivered.

“I need a wee!” declared Mrs Batty.

“You can’t say that,” Pa Baddle warned. “It would be all the same if you were in some children’s book. People in books never do anything of the sort!”

“Well I do need a wee and it’s no good telling me not to say it. Book or no book, if I need it, I say it. So there!” she added for good measure. She stood up. Her joints creaked and cracked and her legs ached. “I’ve been sitting in the damp grass for much too long. I’m all seized up.” She narrowed her eyes suspiciously,

"Why don't you lot need a wee? It hasn't got anything to do with this damp grass has it?"

Pa Baddle crossed his legs and tried to think about something else. Henry looked totally innocent but Boots started staring skywards and whistling nonchalantly, (or so he thought). Actually, he looked as guilty as a biscuit thief with crumbs around his mouth!

Mrs Batty said, Won't be a tick, I'm just going to check out that trailer over there. She pointed toward the edge of a wood where a part laden trailer stood in the shade. Off she went, singing a song that sounded suspiciously like 'trickling down my leg!'

"We can't sit here all morning too. Nothing has happened and I have the feeling that nothing will, except more trailer visits, at least that is, while we continue to follow this particular plan of action. The 'do nowt' way is also more than a touch boring," Henry said while his eyes pleaded with Pa Baddle to do something, ANYTHING!

"What about if we go and see this 'Fast Harling' then?" Pa suggested.

Henry let out a huge sigh of relief. 'Hooray, at last!' he thought.

Shortly, Mrs Batty joined them and they all started to walk up the hill in the direction of the sign labelled Fast Harling. There were no pavements so every time a car screamed past, they all dived into the verge. One car went past six times to get the most out of this unexpectedly fun situation. The driver was forced to stop after six times, purely because he had been laughing so much that he forgot to look where he was going and drove through a hedge and straight into a field.

The weird looking group passed him at the top of the hill and bid him a good morning. The driver shot them a withering glance and continued speaking into his mobile phone, ignoring their presence as best he could, except to note their clothes and mutter "Useless tourists," in a barely concealed sneering voice.

......While Poppy slept, Boris decided it would be best to organise a search party. Being Sadday (when visiting children returned to their world if they were going), people would already be in a quiet mood. Children in Odd were considered to be a privilege, not a right. Losing them to a grouchy, poorly operating world where they would be just about tolerated, left the people of Odd feeling bereft and saddened.

"Bean, could you and Peanut go around and ask some volunteers to meet me at the upside down tree so that we can all search in a methodical way for Boots and Mrs Batty? I have left Poppy a note.

I will take the opposite direction toward the village hall and ask all I meet along the way to do the same. Can you two go right the way up to the funfair?"

The children nodded. Peanut put Flame in her pouch pocket on the front of her sweatshirt. They opened the cottage door and stepped outside into the drizzly rain. "Oh dear," sighed Boris as he noticed the rain. "This is a most unfortunate state of affairs. We haven't had rain here during the day for such a long time. Then it happens twice in as many days. I am feeling more and more that something isn't right. I hope it stops soon, I mustn't get wet." He shrugged and set off toward the village hall.

As they walked along, Peanut stroked Flame's head softly. "Why do you suppose that Boris mustn't get wet?" she asked. Her shoes were getting wet in the long fresh green grass.

"No idea", Bean replied blankly. They walked on in silence for a while, passing a colourful group of people escorting a young boy from 'The World'. They were already heading in the direction of the upside down tree but their sole purpose this morning was to see the lad off on his journey and to wish him well. They all looked sad, but were trying to be brave. Their smiles just didn't reach their eyes.

"It's a strange statement to make though," Bean finally responded. Then he continued, "What do you think has happened to Mrs Batty?"

"Was she okay when she left?" Peanut asked. "Only, I was so enraptured with Flame, I didn't really pay that close attention to how she looked or what she was saying. I feel really guilty about that too, she is such a nice lady. I know she goes on a bit but she has been so kind to us."

They passed the flower fields. The bluebells looked impressive, snuggled into the lush length of the multi-shaded green arms of grass. "She looked alright," Bean shrugged. "She seemed quite happy in herself but she did sound a little worried. Sort of cautious and wary, if you know what I mean." Body language was more Peanuts department than it was his. He wasn't used to being asked an opinion on the topic!

Further along the pathway, they found it to be a lot quieter. The children hardly met anybody at all. Usually it was such a busy route too, even on Sadday. They didn't talk much either. There was a sinking feeling in the air. It felt very similar to the way they had often felt in their own world. Peanut looked up. "Bean," she said slowly, "you don't suppose that something has actually gone wrong with Odd do you?"

Bean stopped in his tracks. "What makes you say that?" he asked.

"It's that feeling you get when you didn't hand in your homework on time or when you suddenly realise that you forgot to return your library books and you know you will be fined. Or..." she searched for the right words "... like when your best loved pet dies." She automatically looked down at her beautiful baby bird. He looked up at her and sang his sweet song.

Finally they met Farmer Jon. "We are getting a search party together." They explained.

"That's good," he told them nodding and stood waiting for them to explain further.

"It's Mrs Batty and Boots."

"Well, you can add Pa Baddle and Henry to the list then. They didn't come from your place last night. Mrs Crimble and her friend Alice are also missing, as of this morning. They went to look for Pa Baddle and Henry and they haven't been seen since." He looked at them both waiting for instruction. Peanut shivered.

The children looked at Farmer Jon, then at each other in shock and disbelief. They all felt really worried. What was happening?

Chapter Four

Deep in the wood the grime-grazer had just eaten half a book. He was on a mission. Eating made him stronger day by day but eating 'Zap the Wizard' books gave him an enormous power boost and made him REALLY strong! He leaned forward and leered at a nesting bird, then he knocked her out of her nest with one swipe of a twig. With a gleeful shout of triumph the rotten coward grabbed one of her eggs and swallowed it whole.

"My baby, my baby!" screeched the poor bird. She flew at the grime-grazer, as near as she dared, desperately trying to distract him from the rest of her eggs. Her heart was thumping loudly in her breast and she was soulfully devastated at the terrible loss of that one baby that would never see Odd.

Laughing out loud, the grime-gazer was already on his way. 'Silly bird,' he thought nastily as he stomped through the damp leaves and undergrowth. Stamping on ants and beetles alike, this nasty creature made his way toward his ultimate goal. Stronger and more cruel than ever before.

......At the upside down tree, animals, craminals, people, children and birds had gathered to search for their missing parties. It came to light that there was a total of ten Odd residents who had disappeared without a trace. The search party spread out and started to trace the path that Mrs Batty and Boots would have taken, alas to no avail. There was absolutely no evidence that they had ever made it this far. Not one hair, button or footprint was found. Nothing at all gave any indication of where they could have gone to. It was puzzling and worrying.

Next, they tried to trace the route that Henry and Pa Baddle would have taken. There was very little talking going on. All that could be heard was the pitter patter of rain as it landed on leaves and ground, and the squelching of shoes in the now muddy pathways. Again, nothing gave the searchers any indication of where their friends and loved ones could have vanished to. It all felt like a really bad dream. The rain continued steadily, adding to the general awful and sickening feeling they had in the pits of their tummies.

All heads were down, steps laboriously trodden, just in case they may strike lucky and find some sort of clue. Bean passed a puddle with a bedraggled copy of 'Zap the Wizard' in it. To give him credit, he did notice it, and he also saw the chewed holes in it, but, he just considered that a slug had rested there a while and feasted. Slugs like damp paper, he reasoned.

......Down at the five crossways, next to the Fast-Harling (heart) sign, a new and oddly assembled group sat shivering on the damp grass. Mrs Crimble, Alice, Lily and Ted, Gus and a dogsheep styled craminal named Shep looked dismally around them. Hats, shorts and walking boots were very much the order of the day as far as dress was concerned. 'Casual' just wouldn't do it justice!

Cars screamed past them. Aeroplanes roared overhead and a tractor chugged down the sloped soil in the field opposite. The hats and shorts brigade just huddled together in silent fear, reading and re-reading the sign, almost like a mantra.

Just over the brow of the hill a tourist type group of hats and shorts were entering a pretty normal looking village. Bungalows lined one side of the road, hamlet styled cottage/houses sat back on the other. "This doesn't look like it's going anywhere," observed Pa Baddle.

"Well, if it is moving, it isn't going nearly as fast as we were led to believe. Perhaps the heart was a clue?" Mrs Batty asked.

They travelled on, past a field with horses, then more houses on the left. On the right of them there was a sign into a road boasting a fox. "I don't think that we need to go up there," Pa Baddle observed. "I must say, I do like the idea of showing you just where the fox lives, that way, if you do want to keep chickens, you would know to set up home seven miles in the opposite direction. Very innovative."

Mrs Batty said she felt tired and that she would rather like a cup of tea. There were some houses on the right, just past where the fox lived. They agreed to go and knock on a door to ask for a cuppa.

In principle it was an excellent idea. In their world, it would indeed be a viable idea. Here however, they were met by an unfortunate tirade of abuse.

Shocked, they continued on their way, rather hurriedly. "Well! In all my life, I have never been called a gypsy," gasped a very hurt Mrs Batty. Boots shook his head and nudged her hand with his head to comfort her. "What is a gypsy anyway?" She looked around her in confusion.

Henry felt really angry. He had never felt angry before. His stomach felt all tense and knotted. He could not believe how rude and disrespectful the occupant had been. A simple 'no' would have sufficed. It was that day that Henry learned an important lesson - he hated injustice.

A little further along the road they found a red brick building with it's door wide open. It seemed like a friendly place and many people were walking around busily.

"Let's try again here?" suggested Boots in his mellow and optimistic way.

They cautiously climbed the two steps and put their heads around the door. There appeared to be a trade going on inside, but nobody was holding a cup and there was no kitchen table. Still, ever hopeful, they joined the end of the queue and shuffled forward with the people in front as they moved forward.

Almost at the counter Henry, who was feeling a little bored, noticed copies of THE book. 'Zap the Wizard and the Land of Odd' sat on the counter. Behind the counter was a box of books that seemed to have been discarded, they all had bite holes in them. Henry frowned and pointed them out to Pa Baddle.

As Pa Baddle and Henry chatted, Boots recalled the copy he had seen in the puddle back in Odd. He shivered, but he didn't know why.

......Boris felt sad. He had no explanation for his friends' disappearance. Just as he thought it could get no worse, he realised that he was soaked through.

The search party had congregated in the village hall. Mrs Bundy and her friend were making tea for everybody so they could try to get warm. "That dreadful damp gets into your very bones," Mrs Bundy thought to herself as she mingled. Her joints ached.

Mrs Bundy could recall when, as a young girl, she had lived in 'The World'. Her parents had often complained of the damp and she had also shivered her way through many a day, but never since going to Odd. It rained at night in Odd, of course it did. She tried to ignore the way their weather had altered and hoped this new weather trend wasn't set to continue.

Sandra had spent the morning cleaning the hall, ready for the meeting. She had placed the chairs in rows and washed all the cups so they could be re-used. There were little posies of wildflowers dotted around the place to help to make it all a little more cheery. It had been rainy and damp when she gathered the flowers and as a result, she was soaked.

As she worked, Sandra could hear Mrs Bundy speaking of when she had been to 'The World'. Sandra had never seen The World. She hadn't even been to the other side of Odd yet.

Mainly she just pottered around doing many of the little tasks that made Odd run so smoothly. She was not alone. There were many people who gave freely of their time for the good of their community, but they were older than Sandra. She was only twenty-two. A little on the plain side but what she lacked in looks, she more than made up for in kindness and loyalty. It had been joked that she would make somebody an excellent wife. But she was usually overlooked for the prettier and louder females. 'That's life!' she thought.

Boris clapped his hands together to call the meeting to attention. "Did anybody find any clues?" he called out, as he looked around the room. There was a general rumble of voices in the hall while the people discussed what they had seen. In unison, they shook their heads. No, they had found nothing at all. "Can anybody recall any of our absent friends saying that they were planning something, or visiting somewhere or even hoping for an adventure?" he asked hopefully. Again, a ripple of voices went around the room, resulting in a mass shaking of heads. No, they could recall nothing, no plans had been heard.

Violet raised her hand and called out "Mrs Batty was going home, I heard her." People nodded their agreement.

Mrs Bundy handed out hot cups of tea and through the sad and thoughtful quietness, a general slurping noise was heard as everybody drank.

Peanut stroked Flame. He blinked up at her. "I don't suppose you know anything do you?" she asked her beautiful baby.

Flame stood up, he was quite wobbly on his legs but he shook himself in preparation and then started the most melancholy haunting tune that Peanut had ever heard in all her life. All eyes turned toward the pair as the song rang out. Then, a really strange thing happened. Flame's eyes seemed to glaze over and a profusion of rainbow colours flickered up, almost like a television. Just for a moment, Peanut thought she saw Mrs Batty!

"Oh my goodness!" she exclaimed as her hand flew over her mouth. Then, convinced that she was wrong, she dismissed what she had seen. However, she still looked over her shoulder, just to check that Mrs Batty wasn't actually stood behind her. There was always a chance that she had seen a reflection in Flame's eyes. Peanut finished her cup of tea with an unsteady hand, then passed the cup back to Mrs Bundy. Bean went to help with the washing up.

Boris next asked the room if any of them had any magic left. "I am greatly concerned at this rain. I'm not sure how many of you can remember back, but it was probably seventy years or more ago that it last rained in Odd during the day. I cannot recall all the circumstances but I do remember that the magic just died. I shall have to look the details up in one of my books. It vaguely comes to me that the combination of damp and lack of sunshine simply drained the magic away."

Old Eric raised his hand. "My magic is gone," he stated quietly. "I thought it was simply needing a little repair or something, but now you mention it, I do recall seventy years ago, the same thing happened to my parents."

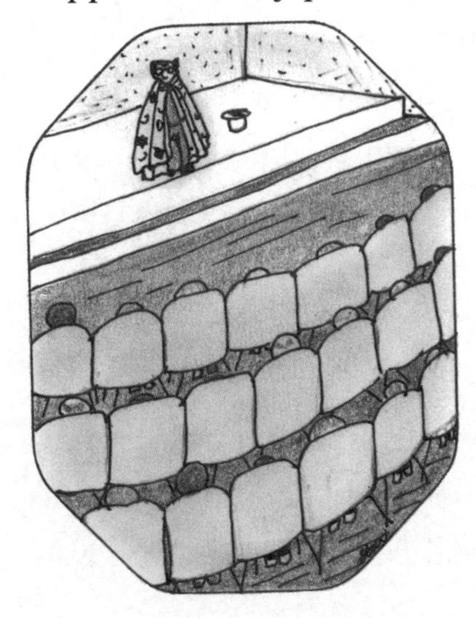

There was such a silence in the hall as everybody contemplated Odd without magic, that you could have heard an ant cough. But old Eric had more to say; "It was shortly after the magic died that my folks died. Dad first, then two weeks later, mum went as well."

The silence grew louder. More hands raised.

"Yes Harold?"

"My magic is gone too and I can also remember losing my parents in a similar way. Is there anything that we can do to turn this situation around?"

"That is THE question right now," agreed Boris, "But WHAT can be the answer? Right everybody, if you hear anything, or find any clues, come and find me at the cottage. Meanwhile, I want you all to check any reference books and History of Odd books that you have."

Boris stared around him. "Diaries will be useful if they are not too painful to read through. We will all meet back here at the same time tomorrow. Try to stay safe, keep dry and keep your wits about you. I know my magic stops when I get soaked through so it may be an idea to get your parasols out and wax them through to waterproof them. Carry them at all times until we are sure that we are home and dry."

Peanut and Bean left the hall with Boris. Some people walked alongside and others went to the cart stop, but there was an eerie silence. Most unusual in Odd.

......Deep, deep in the wood, the grime-grazer sat picking yucky bits from between his toes and sniffing it. He had eaten two entire books and he was feeling a pleasurable surge of energy. He looked around him, leaned over and took a grab at a leafy green shrub. He tore it from the ground, dislodging a nest of woodlice. He stamped on the lot of them, then lay down to contemplate his next move.

The truly frightening thing about his actions was that he was no bigger than the palm of your hand, yet the shrub he had just uprooted was as tall as a car! That was one heck of a lot of power and strength for such a nasty little man to have.

......Once home, Peanut made a quick afternoon tea of cheese sandwiches with salad. She put out biscuits to follow. She didn't want to draw any more attention to the lack of magic that Boris was currently experiencing. After all, it was only a year since he had got his full powers back again. It must be so frustrating to go and lose the lot. She glanced out of the window and watched the rain roll down the window panes.

Bean handed Flame back to Peanut as they all sat down to eat. Boris only managed a few mouthfuls. He was worrying about what to say to Poppy when she awoke.

They didn't have long to wait. Poppy came through the kitchen doorway while they were still eating. She already knew that Mrs Batty hadn't been found. They were all too quiet. If they had found her, she knew there would be a great deal more banter going on. She sat down next to Bean and picked up a lettuce leaf.

Twirling it between finger and thumb she looked from one face to another. Nobody knew what to say.

Boris cleared his throat, but as he went to speak Poppy said "Don't worry. Somehow I just know that she is alright, and she does have Boots with her so I am sure she will be fine."

Boris swallowed another mouthful. "We are going to do everything in our power to find them. There are a few people missing, not just Mrs Batty and Boots. We can only hope that they are all together. I am off to do some research now, but I hope to have more information for you in an hour or two Poppy. Please try not to worry. There are lots of people trying to find them." Boris smiled at Poppy as she nodded at him. She knew she could trust dear old Boris.

"I am going to pop home and see if Mrs Batty and Boots have been back yet. I will return here once I know. We have a book about missing persons and who to contact to trace them. I don't know if it is for Odd or The World, but I can find out while I am there. If it looks as though it will be of any use I will bring it back with me." Poppy said.

She gave them all a hug and slipped through the open kitchen door into the rain. "See you soon." she called back. They could hear her feet splashing through puddles as she ran along the path and out of the gate.

Chapter five

......The Fast Harling sign hadn't altered. It seemed to Lily and Ted that they had been staring up at this sign for weeks when a voice in the air said "Odd!" Then, there was a loud 'Thud!' Old Eric and Mrs Bundy landed in a tangled heap beside them all.

Lily and Ted recoiled in horror, until they realised they had just been joined, albeit in an ungainly fashion, by their great friends from Odd. There followed a great deal of back slapping and talking.

......In Fast Harling mail office, three people and a dog were happily drinking tea. The post mistress was a very kind lady, and despite the overall look of these tourists, she decided to assist them in their hour of need. With smiles and nods she told them all about the camping park in the opposite direction to the path they had taken. Assuring them it was a nice place to visit, she went about her work.

Eventually, they started on their way again. "At least this time, the walk will be mainly down hill," they agreed. The walk didn't seem nearly so daunting now they had drunk their tea.

......The Fast Harling group of eight, nine if

you counted Shep, decided to walk in the opposite direction to Fast Harling (heart). Judging by the speed and noise of the vehicles around here, they didn't wish to visit anywhere faster! Their route took them along a pot-holed, tarmac road. There were no pathways or walkways so they were obliged to leap out of the way of the oncoming traffic. The entire group were a little shocked at the lack of cart stops. They hadn't seen a single one!

Mrs Crimble walked slowly. The damp air was playing havoc with her knee joints and it hurt her to walk. Lily and Ted seemed similarly affected by the damp conditions. "I do hope that we can find somewhere nice to have a bite to eat and get warmed through again," Mrs Crimble said, almost to herself. She hated to complain but her knees did hurt.

Old Eric and Mrs Bundy hadn't quite come to terms with their day's pursuits. One would usually be in his garden and the other would usually be in her house. Falling into this place hadn't done much for their sense of humour. They just walked on in silence, taking it all in while wanting to get out!

Jay, Gus, Alice and Shep walked on a little way ahead. Each time they rounded a corner they hoped to see a shop or café, or even a house would do, but there had been no such luck. There were avenues of trees, more avenues of trees and by small contrast, fields lines with trees and bushes backed with trees.

Finally, they rounded a corner and faced an almost completely straight road "Oh dear!" exclaimed Lily, stopping short. Mrs Crimble walked straight into her. "Ouch!"

"Sorry," she said. Then, "Oh dear indeed. I wonder if we should turn around and go in the opposite direction after all? There doesn't appear to be anything along this road except more trees." She squinted her eyes together, eying the road, "A lot more trees!" she amended.

Ted felt worried too. He didn't like to say anything because he would rather find a way to keep everybody's spirits high. They were already totally lost without them being dejected and scared. "I know," he said, "lets play eye spy!"

"Yeah, lets!" said Jay in his most cutting tone. "Oh do let me start, I spy with my little eye, something beginning with T." Ted hadn't caught the dripping sarcasm and started to try and guess.

"I know, I know, tree!" he said triumphantly.

"Oh yippee, how clever!" sneered Jay. "Let me go again, do. I spy with my little eye, something else beginning with T". Ted began to feel uneasy.

"Alright, so maybe it wasn't such a good idea," he nodded. "But it would have helped to pass the time. "Don't be nasty Jay," begged Alice. "How about we sing a song as we walk, or whistle? Anything really." she shrugged.

Mrs Crimble said, "Where are we Ted? I am really frightened. I don't recognise any of this place and why is everything in such a hurry? Look, even that squirrel moves as though it has had a few too many nuts. Look at it's jerky, hurried movements. Back home they smile up at you from the grass as they lay sunning themselves. Here it looks as though this will be the very last tree they climb or nut they will eat. It is just so odd."

"It is most definitely not Odd." Lily stated. "Odd is a beautiful charming place where the pace of life allows common courtesy and a chance to smell the roses. Here, wherever we may be, all I can smell is Poo."

"It is called dung," Gus interjected helpfully. "They spread it on the fields to make the crops grow."

"Well our crops grow just fine and we don't have to put poo on them." Mrs Crimble observed. She was feeling hot, tired and not very like herself at all.

They continued to walk for a while, gradually growing warmer as the weak sun gained ground. It was almost directly above them now. "It must be mid-day." observed Ted.

"I need a drink and a sit down. I am tired," Gus said. "Look....."

Everybody looked. There in the distance was a figure and he was heading their way. "We can ask where we are," Gus said hopefully, as he stood shielding his eyes.

The group sped up a little to meet him, until finally the cyclist was drawing level.

"Excuse me," called Lily, "Sir, could you tell us where we are?"

"The Chase" called out the frantically pedalling figure as he hurtled past them. The group stared at him in disbelief as he vanished into the distance.

"Are you sure that *was* a boy?" Alice asked. "His shorts were pretty shiny and tight for a boy, so was his t-shirt and what's with the swimming goggles? You would have thought that he was going swimming, not cycling!"

"Maybe he was a girlboy or a fishboy like we are craminals," Shep said. He rather approved of seeing the humans following their behaviour. They usually seemed so 'together' on what they were, seldom had he seen any deviation from it.

"It was a girl," Alice stated in her most authoritive voice.

Having covered about half a mile of straight road, they were about to round the next bend when Ted said "Ah good. There is a sign here on the right, directing us toward a widows house. See, there is even a little picture of it". He pointed at the brown tourist sign. "Perhaps we can get some rest and refreshments here."

Everybody nodded, pleased. They set along the stony track, taking them even further into the trees.

......Boris was having a worrying moment. The more he read of his reference book, the more concerned he became. He was also deeply worried about his current lack of magic. What on Odd was he to do?

It had always been his belief that nobody over 'a certain age' could leave Odd. It had never occurred to him that people as old as Pa Baddle and Mrs Crimble could travel to 'The World'. Now, as he read through the histories of their two worlds, he learned that they actually co-existed on parallel planes. Not only could one not exist without the other, but there were ways for people to travel no matter what age! He had been wrong. Hugely wrong!

He scanned book upon book, trying to find out more about the reasons and circumstances of the elders departures. Just as he thought he was about to discover how it could happen, the book ended or simply referred to it as 'those times'. This wasn't any help whatsoever.

He tried looking up 'those times' but there was no reference to them in any chapter title. It was almost like chasing starlight. You could see it but you could never get near enough to touch it.

He wondered if it were only alluded to simply because it were pure superstition. But then, where had all the magic gone and where had all their friends gone? It was baffling.

Flame had just eaten when Peanut noticed the tiny feathers developing on his pink fluffy wings. They were the brightest shade of red. "His feathers are just like flames aren't they Bean?" she observed. She stroked them. They didn't feel nearly as soft as his pink fluffy down, but would be a great deal more useful, she mused.

Bean leaned over to take a closer look. "He has them growing on his head too, and on his tail. Flight feathers then if they are on his tail." Bean noted. Then he went back to his book. "It says here that the Red Backed Buckle Bum has great magic and can see things." He continued to read the section out to Peanut, "That the parent or carer will be able to share some of these experiences. I wonder what they can mean? Oh wow, look at this one," he pointed one out to Peanut, "it has got really strange eyes."

Peanut looked to where Bean pointed. Sure enough, the bird in the picture had glassy eyes with rainbows shimmering out. "Grief! That's quite scary. I'm glad that Flame doesn't look like that. Don't think it would help much with the parental bonding process."

"Don't be silly, you would still be just as besotted as you are now. You would adore him simply because he was left in your care and he is all soft and fluffy. Girls!" he rolled his eyes in mock despair, grinning. "I wonder if it has stopped raining yet?" He walked over to the door and stared out. "Huh, drizzle, drizzle and more drizzle," he sighed despondently. "Doesn't this place remind you of somewhere?" he asked Peanut.

"Shush! Don't remind me. Let's go for a walk anyway, I could do with stretching my legs and a bit of fresh air wouldn't go amiss either." She stood up. "We haven't been out all day, and it's Myday today."

"What about getting wet? Boris said not to."

"We didn't have any proper magic anyway and we have been wet before. It has never altered anything has it? I am pretty sure that we will be okay."

Bean put his hand out of the doorway to catch a drip or two of rain. They put some coats on. As Peanut was about to go, Flame stretched his wings out and began to sing. Next he flapped his wings as though testing them, then he started the strangest mime, dancing to his own rhythm. Peanut initially wanted to laugh. She set him down on the floor. He wobbled about, still dancing. It looked so funny. But it would have been cruel to laugh. He was obviously in such earnest.

Then, when it became almost too comical *not* to laugh, she noticed his eyes. They had gone weird again. In their reflections she could definitely see Mrs Batty. Not just Mrs Batty, because there along side her stood Boots. "Bean," she cried in a startled voice, "Quick, look!"

Bean had also been suppressing laughter as he stared out into the misty damp land of Odd. With a jolt he swiftly crossed the room in two strides, but before he could look, Flame's eyes had clouded back over, returning to their liquid jet black look again.

"What?" he asked. "What are you looking at?"

"It was his eyes. They were showing me something. Quick, where is your book? He was definitely telling me something. Can these Red Backed Buckle Bums talk?" she asked excitedly. "I am sure I just saw Mrs Batty and Boots. He did exactly the same thing in the hall yesterday but I just thought I was seeing things." She picked up the large reference book and started to flick through the pages.

Turning to the part where they had seen the rainbow coloured eyes, she started to read. It said that the bird's magic was depleted by rainy weather, as was all magic, but their lack of voice would be replaced by visions. Their eyes could serve almost like a television set. The bird would be capable of tuning in to your needs, then displaying the answers for you in their sight!

“I am positive that it was Mrs Batty and Boots. At least we know they are okay. Quick, let’s tell Boris.”

Chapter Six

......Deep in the forest of Odd, the grime-grazer had found a frog. He picked it up and threw it far out into the woodland lake. "Haha! Hahahaha!" He rubbed his hands together in sheer delight and hunted around for another. He kicked twigs and pebbles aside but momentarily, could find no more.

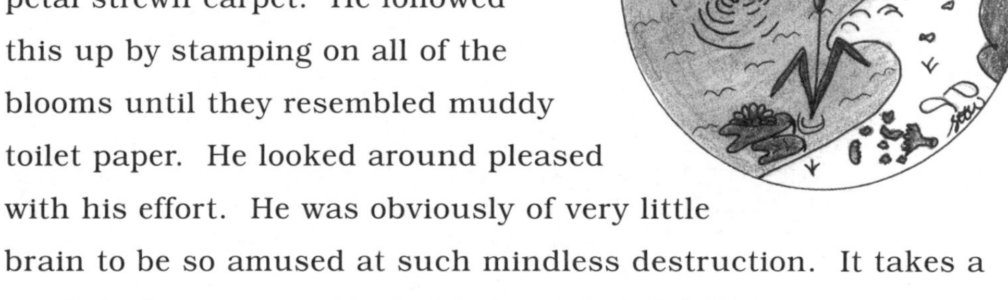

Next he turned his attention to the flowers. Picking up a stick he swiped it back and forth, cutting all the heads from the stems and leaving a petal strewn carpet. He followed this up by stamping on all of the blooms until they resembled muddy toilet paper. He looked around pleased with his effort. He was obviously of very little brain to be so amused at such mindless destruction. It takes a great deal more sense to do kind and helpful things.

The grime-grazer's eyes rested upon a beetle. This he ate in one gulp. When he got to the bin he tipped it over. Rooting through all the smelly contents, he found a glass bottle which he smashed, leaving all the glass for little creatures and children alike to do themselves damage on. He was a very nasty, mindless little character.

Laying in the pile of rubbish there was a discarded magazine article that somebody had screwed into a ball. Initially, the grime-grazer thought there was a fellow grazer on it.

That was what first caught his attention. As he unrolled the page he decided to eat the article instead. He had taken a bite when it dawned on him that the paper didn't look very Oddish.

Spreading the page once more he started to read, slowly. (Grime-grazers are not very literate. They tended to rely more upon being nasty and oafish so had precious little patience for reading). But this page interested him. It could be a way to get to 'The World'.

......Myday was usually the day people used to do something they wanted to do for themselves, often alone. Things such as reading, hobbies and solo pursuits were often in progress throughout this day. Boris was doing just that. He had almost buried himself in books as he searched through one, then another in his desperate bid to find some relevant information.

He too had discovered something about the Red Backed Buckle Bum and he was terrified. Now he knew why so many people had lost their lives. Now he knew why there was such a mystery about these birds. But he had seen them hatch previously. Never had he witnessed anything untoward. He must have seen eighty or more of this variety hatch.

According to this book, every one in a hundred hatchings contained a nasty surprise.

Worse than a virus, stronger and nastier than anything he had known could exist here in Odd and, indeed, The World! If it got enough strength together to get there, that is!

A handful of these awful creatures were already at large in the world. They had rain during the day. Boris knew this but what he hadn't realised was that it was because of the vicious grime-grazers. This one would also be heading toward The World!

Boris felt sick. He cast his mind back. He hadn't seen any sign of violence at Flames hatching had he? Then it dawned on him. The ACTUAL hatching had gone by without a witness! Surely, he questioned, there would have been more mess? He tried to recall, where the eggshell had been when he entered the kitchen? An image of the kitchen came to him momentarily and in a flash he remembered that was the very day it had started to rain. The very day... the people had started to vanish. His tummy churned, as he recalled it to be THE DAY THAT IT ALL STARTED TO GO WRONG!

He started to run toward the kitchen. He had to warn the children. Grief, was it only three days ago that this had all started. It felt like much longer without the sunshine. He had an awful suspicion that he knew what else had been contained within Flame's egg with Flame... a... a... he didn't want to contemplate it. It was too dreadful for words. He just KNEW that the un-witnessed hatching had contained a Grime-grazer!

As Boris ran through the corridor, Peanut was running toward the study and CRASH!

They ran full pelt into each other. Boris staggered backwards, books flying from his arms. Peanut flew up and bounced none too bouncily into the wall and sort of slithered down it, to the floor.

"Ow, argh, my, oh ow!" She started. Boris went immediately to help her up.

"Are you okay little one? I'm so sorry Peanut, I wasn't looking where I was going. Here," he offered her his hand, "let me help you up."

"I'm alright Boris, don't worry," she said rubbing her backside where she had sat suddenly upon it. Together they picked up the books and headed back toward the kitchen. Boris made some tea, manually. Once they were all sat around the table, he started to tell the children what he had learned. Bean still had his coat on.

"Now then children. It is really important that you try to recall the afternoon when Flame hatched." Boris looked gravely from Bean to Peanut. "What did you notice when you first entered the kitchen? Was Flame fully or part hatched? Where was the Egg?" Peanut looked down at Flame. Bean looked at Peanut.

"How did the egg hatch? Did it rock gently or did it shake and bounce?" Boris insisted.

"No, it definitely rocked. It was mesmerising. I watched it until Bean called me to go outside to play on the swing." She frowned, "No actually, that isn't totally true," she corrected herself. "It did shake in between rocking, not all the time though, just every now and again. Why, does that matter?" Her frown deepened, she was worried that her baby may be defective in some way. She felt very protective towards him. Sweet thing!

"What else, Peanut? Bean? What can you remember? This is really important. Where was the eggshell?" he repeated. "Where was the bird, what else did you see?"

Bean looked up at the ceiling and noticed an excellent spider's web with bead work on it. "Yes, I remember," he said. "The bird was looking really cute in the middle of the table. The shell was all around him."

"It was across the floor too," Peanut recalled. "We picked it all up, do you remember?" She turned to Bean for his agreement. "Why does it matter? What does it mean? Does Flame have a split personality or something?" She hugged Flame closer to her, almost as though a hug would make it all better!

"No, it is a lot worse than that." Boris said quietly.

Peanuts face was ashen. She stared silently at Boris, waiting for her world to fall apart.

There was no easy way to say it. "If I am right, and honestly I would rather not be, but if I am, we are all in serious trouble. Odd could be about to die, and us with it." The silence in that little cottage kitchen went on and on.

Peanut could bare it no more, "Why? Because of Flame? I won't let you harm him if that's your answer to this stupid news. He wouldn't hurt a fly!" she cried.

"No Peanut. The problem is that I don't think Flame was the only thing to come out of Flame's egg. My book tells me that for every hundred hatchings, one egg contains the dreadful and deadly creature known as a Grime-grazer."

"Ugh! It sounds horrible, but what is it? How can it hatch out of the same egg? That's impossible. If it did, then where is it?" Bean asked.

"It IS horrible. That is what I am telling you! It is a creature that feeds on nastiness and evilness. It undoes the good and replaces it with bad. Where there is life, it causes death. Where there is light, it causes dark. If there is sun, it will make rain. Health turns to illness and laughter to sadness. Love turns to hate and all around will be destruction."

Boris continued. "The Grime-grazer's mission is to destroy beauty and leave only ugliness in all its varying degrees. Where is it? That is a good question, I am almost certain that one was born with Flame and we must find it, and soon!"
"But Flame is so sweet and kind, it cannot be possible. Surely Flame wouldn't have survived being holed up with such a terrible thing?" Peanut protested.

"Yes, but that is the worst thing. The nicer the co-existent of the egg, the more evil the grime-grazer. This is terrible. Don't you remember? It started to rain the moment that Flame was born. It poured down when he sang."

"But Flame wouldn't do that." Peanut was almost in tears. She was frightened that Boris was about to tell her that the only thing that could stop the grime-grazer was to destroy Flame.

"No, you don't understand," Boris countered. "It is not Flames fault. The grime-grazer exists now, separately to Flame. Flame may even be able to help us but it certainly isn't his fault. He is as much a victim of the situation as we all are. The thing is, we have GOT to find this thing and we have got to stop it. Don't you recall the world you left behind? Do you not realise what infected it?"

Just then there was a knock at the door. They all jumped. "It's only me," grinned Poppy as she walked in and saw all the startled faces. She had returned from her trip to Mrs Batty's cottage.

“They haven’t been back,” she told them, “but I have the book about missing persons with me, it may be of some use.” She sat down next to Peanut.

“There are no less than six grime-grazers on the loose in ‘The World’, and those are the ones we are aware of.” Boris told them. “Their arrivals span back over the last few hundred years. So far, it is only the female grime-grazers that have managed to hatch and escape Odd. I suspect they are slightly more keen, on the basis that they are looking to breed. Now, for the first time in the history of Odd, they stand a chance. It is my belief that the grime-grazer that hatched in our own kitchen is indeed a male.”

“Why do you think it is male Boris?” Bean asked.

“You told us that the discarded shell had reached as far as the door. A female would not have the strength at hatching to throw the shell that far, not even in rage.”

“What is a grime-grazer?” Poppy interrupted.

“He thinks a nasty thing hatched with Flame,” Peanut whispered. “I’ll tell you later.” Boris nodded and went on;
“As you so cleverly observe Peanut, Flame is the sweetest and

most enchanting Red Backed Buckle Bum ever to hatch. This means that by contrast, not only do we have a male but we are dealing with the worst ever grime-grazer. Already we are without magic, I dread to think what lies ahead of us. We have got to act quickly and we will need to stay on our toes."

"Just think of what could happen if this one gets to The World. It will be dangerous enough if he stays here, but if he gets the chance to breed it will be the end of Odd, the end of The World and the end of us all." Boris leapt about in his agitation. His arms flying around as he tried and tried again to conjure up some magic. Finally, defeated he sat down again. "Its no good," he sighed. "Even though I am dry now, my cloak still isn't working. I am useless. I have no magic and without it I am just... an old man."

"That's not true Boris. Please don't feel bad, we think you are brilliant even without magic." The children all nodded.

"What shall we do Boris?" Bean asked. "Is there anything that can help us? What about the people who are already missing. Which do we need to work on first?"

"Quite right lad, we need a plan. We will need everybody to help and pull together on this one. This thing is far too great to struggle with alone. The more people that are aware, the less likely anybody is to make a mistake or miss a clue. We must call a meeting. You never know, perhaps our friends have found a magic stash or maybe our friends have already been found. Do you still have the eggshell Peanut?"

"Yes Boris, we cleared it into a shoebox. I wanted to keep it so I can show Flame when he is older." Peanut went to fetch it from under her bed.

Bean took a moment to explain to Poppy all that had been discovered. She was horrified.

"By looking at the shell we will be able to check for certain what we are dealing with here." Boris told them. "Any green fluff or hair indicated a female grime-grazer. If it is blue, it's a male. I would rather not find anything but I just know I will, and I feel certain already it will be blue."

Sure enough, when Peanut returned, they all stared into the box. There on the very edges of two pieces of shell was Flame's pink and something else's blue.

"Oh pants!" breathed Bean. They all looked at Boris.

"Right, let me tell you what NOT to do. Do NOT chase this thing if you see it. Do NOT even let it know that you have seen it. Even if it dances up and down in front of you, pretend it is invisible.

There is nothing that you can do to one of these creatures that will harm it. It's main mission in life is to be evil and cruel. He will stop at nothing and you are the ones who will get hurt." Boris looked sternly round the table at each child, emphasising his point.

"Our only chances lay in either magic, or outwitting it. Any sightings, let me know. I am off to print some urgent flyers. Perhaps you three can get them out this afternoon as soon as they are ready? The meeting can be first thing tomorrow. Try not to worry but please be careful."

The children went for a quick walk in the rain. Even Poppy, despite just returning from the cottage. She didn't feel able to sit still now!

It dawned on Peanut that Odd was growing swiftly more like The World every minute. She shivered. Her feet were wet and there was no hint of the previously ever-present sunshine. She wanted more than anything to be able to help Boris put it all right. She hugged Flame closer to her as she walked, feeling responsible for all the dreadful things that were happening now. It was a nasty feeling.

Chapter Seven

. . . Mrs Batty, Boots, Pa Baddle and Henry all travelled toward the camping site in the West of Fast-Harling (heart), as the lovely post-mistress had directed. She had told them it was peaceful there. She gave them some directions and bottled water before they set out, in case they grew thirsty again on their journey. She had also wished them all a lovely holiday.

"What is a tourist?" Mrs Batty asked. "Oh my, I think I can smell spring onions, my favourite," she smiled. "What's a holiday?" she mused. They walked along for a while in companionable silence, passing the lunatic driver with a cheery wave. They thought he was talking to himself but he was in fact still attempting to get help from the 'roadside recovery' of his choice.

Apparently, because he was no longer on the roadside, he was no longer their problem. He had been screaming at them for almost half an hour when the operator made a truly snide comment about him not having 'middle of the field assistance.' For the lunatic motorist, this was just about the last straw. He threw his mobile phone over the hedge. It landed at Pa Baddle's feet as he walked.

Pa Baddle bent down and picked up the little silver box. He tried very hard to keep an open mind, but even he was surprised that this place they called the world had such huge and dangerous missiles contained within its rain. He made a mental note to watch the sky a lot more carefully in the future, it could obviously be a very dangerous thing!

Curious, he opened the lid of the missile to inspect it further and noticed a lot of numbers and pictures. Just as he was about to press the smiley one, the 'thing' started to make a strange noise. He hastily closed the lid and put the box deep into one of his coat pockets.

Pa Baddle was in fact the only member of the visitors from Odd to be wearing a coat. He always wore a coat. It was always the same one. It smelt like it was always the same one too! Black, long, unbuttoned and slightly tattered. With shorts and walking boots he had unwittingly stumbled across the correct dress code for Fast Harling visitors. He fitted in very well.

Boots was picking up some very interesting scents as they walked along. Every now and again he got the distinct whiff of Pa Baddle's coat, then dung, then Mrs Crimble? No, surely not. Now, if the like of Mrs Crimble were here, all would be well. Mrs Batty and Mrs Crimble were the absolute best cooks in all of Odd. Coo, what a feast they could have if both of these fine ladies got together on it.

Henry's shoes hurt. He wasn't used to walking on solid roads and his shoes were quite thin soled. He stayed next to Boots as they walked, mindful that he was lucky to be the youngest amid them and aware that he was probably faring a great deal better than the older members of the group.

......At the widows house Old Eric was mighty surprised to see a very neat, self-contained lake. It was rectangular in shape and azure blue in colour. Clearer than any lake he had ever seen before and he fancied a swim in it.

Alice was similarly impressed, although, she was slightly disturbed by the lack of laughing children, animals and craminals, but reminded herself that this place was not at all like Odd anyway. To be honest, nothing would really surprise her now.

Shep was the first one into the water, but then he had no clothes to take off. Ted was next. He didn't bother to stop and take off any clothes anyway. Mrs Bundy, Old Eric and Mrs Crimble all sat along the edge and dangled their hot sore feet in the water. They took a look around while they chatted.

Not far from the contained lake (better known as a swimming pool) there stood the depicted 'Widows House.' It looked quite large but it couldn't have that many rooms Mrs Bundy surmised, (incorrectly) because it looked as though their guests had to bring their own bed pods. The bed pods were scattered all around the field. They had wheels! Mrs Bundy guessed that these people hadn't been certain of a welcome or a room prior to their arrival.

She wondered if she should go and introduce herself to the widow. She could explain how good she was at cooking and how willing she was to help. There must be more than a hundred people for the poor lady to cater for. She was obviously a popular lady, no wonder she didn't make it obvious that she would welcome them all, she reasoned. (Incorrectly again!)

The group agreed. It would be a friendly thing to do to offer assistance. So it came about. Within moments of making the acquaintance of their host, Old Eric was mowing the field and Mrs Crimble and Mrs Bundy were in the kitchen. They hadn't realised just how short of willing workers they were in these parts!

......Peanut, Poppy and Bean returned to the cottage and made a plate of sandwiches for lunch, placing them on the table, Peanut went to find Boris. He was pleased to see her, and the flyers were all ready to be delivered. They carried them to the doorway for delivery after lunch.

"Did you spot anything while you were out and about?" Boris asked the children. They shook their heads.

Poppy said, "Actually, it may not be anything, but I noticed our walk was very quiet. I didn't hear anything. Not even the birds were singing. I thought it was quite odd as we walked along but I couldn't work out why. I mean, rain is odd in itself so the eerie silence didn't strike me as odd until n......" BANG! A puff of smoke swirled up from where Poppy had been sitting. They all stared in horror as they realised that Poppy had simply disappeared.

"Oh grief!" Bean stood up in alarm.

"Goodness!" Peanut also jumped up in her shock.

Boris put his hand to his head. "That's it!" he shouted, banging his fist on the table. "I knew there must be a way!" He looked triumphantly at the children, their faces white with shock.

"There is *some* magic working. You have just witnessed it. That is where Mrs Batty, Pa Baddle and the rest have gone to. Don't you see? They all said 'Odd' three times!"

"But you said it doesn't work if you are over a certain age," Bean reminded him. "Pa Baddle is old and Mrs Batty is positively ancient. There is no way they could have vanished that way."

"Yes, this is true, but you have to remember that we are in the clutches of a grime-grazer. They undo all the good. It is for the good of everybody that our elders may only travel while young. Else they may just decide to start meddling. They could travel to The World and start fixing it. Can you imagine what would happen then?"

"Most of them haven't any understanding of The World, let alone the things in it. No, they are meant to travel while young. The main reason the grime-grazer would turn this rule on its head is so that HE can get to The World." Boris stated. He felt really good now he had at least worked out that his missing friends were more than likely safe. He continued;

"That grime-grazer will be watching and learning. Then, once he has worked out a way of getting out of Odd he will be back and forth until he has destroyed both places." Realisation dawned again. "Ohhhhhhhhh!" he groaned. "This is disastrous. He is working a lot quicker than I gave him credit for. He is only a few days old!" Boris rubbed his forehead in distraction. Perplexed he looked at Peanut and Bean. "What can we do?" he asked them, hunching his shoulders in a wave of despondency.

"Don't worry Boris, maybe there is a lot we can do. What about Flame? He grows stronger every day. If what you say about 'reverses' is true, then Flame could be our answer to everything." Then Peanut added, "Somehow! Bean, pass me that book will you?" She held her hand out for the book. "We need to find out just how good these little creatures really are."

......Poppy landed at the Fast Harling (heart) sign. She looked up in surprise.

"Wow, this place must rock!" she said out loud as she took in the flatness of her surroundings. She appeared to be stood next to the only hill for miles around. She squinted into the distance where the flat earth met flat sky in a hazy abstract, then she turned back to the hill up to Fast Harling.

"Well, I am NOT climbing any hill when there is no need." Turning back toward the road she stood upon, she noted with a grimace a sign showing Indian tents (worrying) but set off towards them at a gentle trot. "May as well find them before they find me." she laughed. It occurred to her that she didn't recognise any of these places. She was working out where she wasn't anyway. Not Yorkshire, not hilly enough. she thought. Then, "Not Odd, its not busy enough," she reasoned.

After a while she passed a huge pile of manure. "Horses by the look of it," she guessed. "And fresh too, by the smell of it!"

As she rounded a bend she saw another sign. This one pointed to a Harling that wasn't fast (heart). She jogged on until she saw a sign to the Indian tents and a widows house. It had to be a camping site.

Drawing nearer, she could hear a lot of laughter and something smelled rather tasty too. Around the last corner, just past a huge tree, Poppy recognised a figure as he sailed by her on a bicycle. "Pa Baddle!" she exclaimed in shock. "Then I AM still in Odd?"

she asked in amazement.

Then she spotted Alice. She was wandering around with a drinks tray. Her cheeks were looking suspiciously red, almost like she had sampled some of the glasses she carried. "Alice?" she asked, in shocked disbelief.

Next, she noticed Boots and Shep giving the toddlers rides around the field. "What is going on?" she asked puzzled. She stood by the huge oak tree, lifted her right arm to scratch her head and just as she was saying "Well I never," she vanished!

Pa Baddle looked back to where she had stood. He was a bit concerned, looking left and then right for her. He went to where she had stood, to check she hadn't gone behind the tree. No, no sign of her. He scratched his head with his right arm. "Well I never!" he sighed. Then he too vanished!

Alice looked down at the empty glass on her tray, then back at the spot where she had seen Poppy, then NOT seen Poppy. Then she had seen Pa Baddle and next could no longer see Pa Baddle and felt a bit grim. "I think I had better have a lie down, it has all been a bit too much for me." she slurred. She looked back at the empty glass... "Much too much," she amended. She went back to the house.

......Flame stretched his wings. He was feeling surges of power flowing through his veins. He needed to travel. He wanted to look around and smell the smells. He wanted to hear the sounds and see the colours.

Instinct was taking him and carrying him. No! Actually, Peanut was carrying him. She and Bean were out delivering the leaflets calling everybody to a meeting. Then, quite unexpectedly they bumped into Poppy. "Hello," they greeted her in unison. "Do you want to help deliver these? ... Hang on, aren't you missing?"

"I was. You will never guess, I know where everybody is. I have seen them. It was amazing. I had just spotted Old Eric floating on his back on a lilo in the pool, sipping a pina colada, when somehow, I am back here. I am not really sure what happened. It was all a bit surreal!"

"You're telling me its surreal. One minute you're gone, next you are right here. All the rules are gone and people are popping in and out without a by your leave or thank you." Bean looked exasperated." You have got to keep your voice down Poppy, there are possible ears and we don't want them hearing what you have just said. In fact, we don't want them hearing anything," he added in a whisper.

"Possible ears? What on Odd do you mean? It sounds terrible. Is it catching? Oh," she nodded as realisation dawned on her. "Yes, I see." She mimed a squidgy faced little man, stomping, then stopped, realising she could be putting them all in danger.
They all continued along the track. Flame was very alert. His

ears turned first one way, then the other, gathering information from all around. In fact, all his senses were alert.
He felt ready for something, though he didn't know what.

Bean looked down at the ground to negotiate puddles and slippery patches of mud. His eyes spotted something black and shiny.
"Look!" He stooped down and picked up a button. This is from Pa Baddle's coat, he said.
WHUMP! Pa Baddle landed in front of them all, none too elegantly.

"Where's my bike gone?" he asked, totally disappointed. He sat with his arms out in front of him, still clutching the imaginary handlebars, toes seeking pedals and legs astride thin air. Then he realised who he was looking at. "Goodness! It's you. Hello, hello," he beamed, all happy once more. "Well I never, am I back in Odd? I must say that IS clever!"

The children gathered around in excitement. "This is brilliant," Peanut laughed. "Are the rest with you?" she asked, looking skyward.

"Yes," Pa Baddle nodded... "No" he amended. "They were. We were all at this amazing place. Between you and me, the people were really strange. Nothing too untoward but I suspect they are taking too many pills. Is that my button young man?" he asked Bean as he spotted his button being rolled between finger and thumb.

"Yes, I thought it may be a clue. Is that how it all works then? If I have something of yours I can call you back from wherever?"
"Don't know." Pa Baddle scratched his nose and looked puzzled.

"No, that's not it," Poppy said. "Unless you had something of mine?" she looked at Peanut and Bean for confirmation.

"No, we didn't." They shook their heads.

"No, that's not it, I remember now," said Pa Baddle triumphanty, pocketing the button as he spoke. It clinked against something as it went in. He was just about to tell them what had happened to bring them both back when Peanut put her finger to her lips and said "Shush! Don't say it. Not here!" She looked around them. "Remember the ears?"

Pa Baddle looked worried and clutched at his ears. All the same, he stopped what he was saying, which was just as well.

"Come on, let's get these leaflets delivered before tea. Mind what you say and keep your eyes open," insisted Bean.

As the children splashed along, Flame was listening to a familiar sound far in the distance. A terrible growly noise. A sick feeling hit his stomach as he realised just what it was that he could hear. Or should I say WHO it was he could hear!

That surging feeling rose up in him again and he breathed deeply. He knew what the sound was and he didn't like it one little bit. THE GRIME-GRAZER! Flame knew it was that creature's fault that it perpetually rained, that the magic was gone so he couldn't speak. The newly grown plume of beautiful red feathers stood up like a magnificent crown on Flames head. He opened his beak and sang and sang for all he was worth. Then he listened.

......The grime-grazer stopped suddenly in his tracks. That terrible sound, that awful yucky malignant sound. It made him ANGRY! He tore up a sapling and threw it to the ground, watching as its exposed roots bounced up and down from the jolt of hitting the ground. Earth fell in clods around it - and still the noise went on.

"ARRRGGGGGGGGHHHHH!" He screamed, clutching his head, stooping as though still carrying the tree.
He held his ears, dropping the interesting article that he had been slowly reading. Still clutching his ears, he bent his knees, the noise went on and on. Staggering around he finally fell to the ground.

......Flame lifted his head. He could no longer hear that noise.

The grime-grazer had stopped. The children and Pa Baddle looked at Flame in total adoration. "What beautiful music Isn't he brilliant?" Peanut stroked him proudly. "He is so clever. When he is older I wonder if his plume will stay like that all the time," she said. With the exception of Flame, they were all totally unaware of the proximity of the grime-grazer.

"According to the book, the plume is an early warning system," Bean said slowly, looking all around him. "But nothing else has happened yet so he must simply be testing it out." He said hopefully. "Come on, lets get this finished and get home."

......The grime-grazer slowly took his hands away from his ears. The terrible noise had stopped. He stood up crossly and stamped on a snail for good measure. "Grrr," he growled. Stooping to collect his precious piece of paper, he stuffed it into his 'pocket' made from a knotted rag and set out to find shelter for the fast approaching night.

Chapter Eight

Once back at the cottage, task completed, they all shared a supper of hot toasted crumpets, oozing with butter, and steaming mugs of hot chocolate and tea. It had felt good to get out and DO something and even better to have some of their loved ones home again. Boris was insistent that they needed a plan. But, as it happens, he wasn't much good at making plans, none of them were.

Pa Baddle explained to the children what had happened while he was away and how he thought he had returned. None of them could believe it was simply a matter of standing next to an oak tree and scratching your head while saying, "Well I never."

"If it were THAT easy, they would all be here by now," Bean said with total conviction.

Similarly, when Boris explained to Pa Baddle how it was they had all managed to leave Odd in the first place, Pa Baddle said he found it pretty hard to believe.

"But one thing is for sure," imparted Boris, "If it is this simple to flit to and from the different places, it won't be too long before the grime-grazer finds out. He will soon be doing this for himself. Remember there are six good reasons awaiting him in The World! We must not let it happen."

They were all agreed. They must NOT let it happen! It seemed like a good plan, but a little too basic to have any effect on the grime-grazer at large!

“Does he know there are more of his kind out there already waiting?” asked Peanut.

“No, probably not, but he will be instinct driven. The need to survive is very strong. Never underestimate what a creature will do to survive. In Odd, he would have difficulty surviving beyond a year. He will stand out like a sore thumb here. But in The World there are lots of things to hide him. By the time he is three months old, he will be just about mature.”

Pa Baddle was taking all this in as though it were an every day occurance, but then not much phased Pa Baddle!

“They develop at the same speed as the Red Backed Buckle Bum,” Boris went on. “This is why their eggs make such good hosts for them to get into. Plus, being large and bright red, the eggs are also really easy to spot and quite roomy once you are in.”

“How can the grime-grazer get into an egg? The shell is solid isn’t it?”

“Good question Poppy, but no! According to the reference books I have been reading, the shell is just as porous as any other egg. When a grime-grazer is little, he is minuscule. Actually, despite the amount of destruction he is capable of, he is still only tiny even when fully developed. He won't grow any bigger than he is at three months. When a grime-grazer finds a host egg, it is only a spore floating on the air current in the warm breeze. The spore is almost invisible to the naked eye. It floats down to the bright red egg and lands upon it. Next it very cleverly releases a tiny amount of acid which dissolves a single pore of the egg and allows him entry. Then he is incorporated into the centre of the egg and grows alongside the chick."

"Grief!" yawned Peanut.

"They hatch together, often a day too early for the chick. This means that the chick will be less alert and simply unable to do anything other than try to survive. The grime-grazer has the ideal situation. He wouldn't wish to be stopped. After a year, if he hasn't found a mate, he will gradually disintegrate and return to spore, to float around again in search of another Red Backed Buckle Bum's egg. They can remain floating for years."

"In the system of things, there are ninety-nine grime-grazer free hatchings per hundred. Is it any wonder that the Red Backed Buckle Bum straps her egg to her back the second it is laid, then runs like fury to the person she believes will be trusty enough to care for her baby. She is desperate not to be the bringer of the grime-grazer. This is the only way she can think of to keep her egg safe."

Peanut fed Flame some of her toasted crumpet. He was managing to peck quite easily now. He seemed to be listening to the conversation and taking it all in.

"Poor you," she said, stroking his head. "You would be able to join in and talk if it weren't for the grime-grazer. I am so sorry. It is me who has let you down by not being as worthy as your mother thought me to be."

"That's not true Peanut. The grime-grazer would already have been in the egg by the time you got it. Perhaps we could design a papoose style carrier for future generations of egg carriers. It would make it a lot less easy to spot. Now, how are we to stop this nasty creature from destroying us? Has anybody got any ideas?" Boris asked in desperation.

"One thing is for certain, it has to be easier to catch him here in Odd. We know the territory but he is still only learning," Bean said.

"Good point. But how?"

"I don't suppose a net would work would it?" Poppy suggested.

"We could certainly give it a try. What if we set a few traps and kept an eye on them each day? We would have to stay vigilant though. It wouldn't be long before the thing would find a way out again if we left him caught up. He would never fall for the same trick twice." Boris replied.

"Could we lure him? What do they like to eat?" Bean asked.

"Ahh, sadly no. You see they are quite disgusting. They don't care what they eat. The messier or crunchier the better. I wouldn't even like to begin thinking about it. If I said they enjoy a dirty slimy slug, would that tell you all you need to know?

"You are kidding? Surely they can't eat slugs!" Peanut wrinkled her nose up in disgust.

"You forget, that would be the staple diet of a bird. He hatched just the same as any bird, so why be surprised at his diet? He would be just as happy to crawl into a bin and select something thrown away a week before. Honestly, he is not choosy."

"Could he be caught unawares, like if he was asleep or something? Could we sneak up and catch him in our hands?"

"No, definitely not. After eating all that muck and filth. One bite from him and you would be infected with goodness only knows. It could kill you. He would bite you until he draws blood. He doesn't care what he destroys. That is absolutely not the way." Boris explained.

"Although, thinking about it, he does have to sleep. Especially while he is so young. He will be taking lots of day time naps as well as getting a full nights sleep. Have any of you had sight of him yet, or seen a sign that he has been around?" Boris looked around.

"Nothing. I was looking all of today too." Bean replied with disappointment.

"What about when Flame's plume stood up?" offered Peanut.

"The book said it was a warning, but we saw nothing and the plume went flat as soon as Flame had finished his song. I think he was testing it out." Poppy said.

"Where were you when it happened?" asked Boris with interest.

"We were on the edge of the wood, Mrs Batty's end. We walked around the outside so that we could do all the perimeter homes. There aren't any houses in the middle of the woods so there didn't seem any point in going in." Bean answered.

"I have a hunch that the grime-grazer wasn't very far away." Boris nodded slowly, tufts of silver hair bobbing up and down as he did so.

Flame nodded in excitement. His eyes glazed over and there in the shininess of his huge black pupils was a very clear picture of the grime-grazer, curled up on a bed of fallen leaves. There was something in the creature's hand, but Peanut couldn't see it close enough to work out what it was. "Look!" she gasped, frantically pointing. Boris and Bean both caught sight of the vision before Flame closed his eyes and began to sleep peacefully.

"Now, this is clever." Boris smiled. "Flame knows exactly where the grime-grazer is and he can show us. This is a breakthrough. So we have some hope. But, it is late and we must sleep. Tomorrow is Ourday and the meeting is shortly after breakfast. Pa Baddle, you must make full use of one of our guestrooms for tonight. Get some rest and you will be all the better to see Ma Baddle and the children in the morning." Boris opened the door to the stairs, standing back to allow everybody to precede him. He was very tired indeed.

......At the widows house, there was great merriment. Alice was really good at her job and everybody's cheeks were glowing. Lily and Ted were in charge of the entertainment so there was a huge train of people dancing the conga around the field.

Old Eric was sat with his back against a tree, strumming on a battered guitar and crooning songs that he made up as he went along. He thought he was really good. This was lucky, nobody else was going to encourage him, so a good self-esteem was needed!

Mrs Bundy and Mrs Crimble had fed everybody so well that they had been crowned cooks of the year and were being treated like minor celebrities. Mrs Bundy had started quite a lucrative pastime of telling people their fortunes. She had been doing this for years back home, but whereas the people back home just got all huffy, here they actually paid her for it! She was quite baffled by this behaviour but understandably delighted.

Jay and Gus had been having fun too. They were busy driving people's cars. To anybody watching, only the top of a head and a pair of eyes were visible over the dashboard as the car kangaroo'd around, stopping in unlikely places, such as the river. Still, nobody seemed to mind that evening and by morning Jay and Gus were nowhere to be seen, so could not possibly be held responsible.

Shep and Boots were snoring under the big kitchen table, pleasantly full and dreaming of Odd, where there was no hot tarmac to burn their paws.

......At the meeting there was uproar in the hall. Loud talking and rumbling of chairs as people manoeuvred them around so they could sit together, or apart, depending on their preference.

When Ma Baddle and the children saw Pa Baddle, well, you could have heard the cheers from miles away! It was a good start to a difficult meeting. Each of them had questions; Where had he been? Where were the others? Were they safe? How did he get there? Etc.

Eventually, Boris took control of the situation and headed toward the stage. He stood there in front of all the lovely people of Odd and raised his hands for silence. When the noise had stopped he started to speak;

“Friends, we have good news and also some bad, but do not be alarmed. We are together and must keep on our guard. Firstly, may I start with an apology. Due to the weather, I am a changed man. I have no magic. So I am deeply sorry but I am unable to intervene in my usual way. We are going to all be pretty dependent upon our wit’s, unless anybody here can help. Does anybody have any magic?”

There was an initial silence but then a little lad named Steven put his hand up. “I still have a Birthday wish if you think it will help?”

Boris looked down at his feet. As always, the kindness of these people humbled him. He was deeply touched by the offer and had to swallow twice to shift the lump that had formed in his throat.

“Thank you, you are very kind. I will accept your offer in the spirit it has been given. But, we will only use the wish if we have to. I am sure there will be a way to repay you for volunteering something that we all know to be very special to you."

Everybody in the hall applauded. Steven went bright red with embarrassment. The meeting continued, questions were asked and answered.

Two other children offered their wishes left over from using the Super-Zappers. These were also graciously accepted. Boris took care to explain about the grime-grazer. He told them how some of the travelling rules had altered and that they mustn't repeat how odd things were three times, for fear of vanishing.

He went on to explain how people were managing to come back again, simply by standing near the oak tree at the widows house in the woods of the World and scratching their heads with the right hand while saying, "Well I never."

Everybody agreed that a rescue squad should be dispatched to gather their missing persons. This was going to be so much easier than the first option which entailed an army going by the name of Sally! (Poppy had been researching missing persons in her book but had failed to grasp the basic details. Apparently Sally could check all her records!) There were lots of helpful arms raised at this point. Everybody had a musical record or two that they felt could be looked at. Boris declined politely, feeling more than a shred of despair!

Boris drew the grime-grazer on a chalk board to allow everybody to see exactly what to look out for. He told them where they suspected the creature was hiding, though he didn't explain at this point about Flame's visions.

There were a lot of suggestions on who should attempt the rescue squad and who should track down the grime-grazer. Nearly everybody wanted to be the rescue squad. Only one man put his hand up to tackle the foul evil hairy blue-grey man, and then only because he had misheard what he was volunteering for. Boris didn't blame them either!

Sadly, when the meeting commenced, nobody had checked who was attending. The meeting went ahead just as everything else did in Odd. Usually this would be fine, but on this particular day, the one day when everything really needed to be fine, it was not.

There was one person there who nobody would have wanted to attend, if indeed they had realised. Right at the back of the hall, wearing a big brown overcoat and a floppy blue hat (courtesy of a scarecrow), sat a stranger. He sort of slumped in the chair, almost as if he knew he would not be welcome.

This stranger was very interested in the travelling information though. Very interested indeed. At the end of the meeting, when everybody was handed a cup of tea, coffee or hot chocolate, he took his cup with a small hairy blue-grey hand.

Chapter Nine

Flame had been feeling surges throughout the meeting. He was having a huge problem in containing the terrible feelings welling up inside of him. He had that sort of feeling of being watched and being in danger. The plume of deep red feathers stood upright. Peanut stroked them during the entire meeting, but they stayed up.

It was really eerie but Peanut was feeling very ill at ease. A few times she looked around her in the hall to see why, but there was no indication of anything being amiss, so she put it down to the general air of worry that had infiltrated Odd.

Also, Peanut really wanted to be amid those who went to get Mrs Batty, she missed her greatly. During her year in Odd, Mrs Batty had become almost like a mother to her, cooking fine things to eat, doing sewing together, chatting and being really good company for each other. Poppy was lost without her and Peanut could easily understand why.

They couldn't lose so many wonderful people. Think of all the skills these folk had between them. They would be losing such fine friends and teachers if they lost them for good. Poppy was grateful to know how to bring them back. Let's just hope that they want to come!

One person was very unhappy during the meeting. It was the owl who had actually seen the grime-grazer but pretended that he hadn't. He had rested for three days and now had to accept that the grime-grazer did actually exist. If he had been a little more honest at the start, the destruction at the centre of the forest may not have been so complete.

One bird was totally devastated by the loss of her egg. When they all heard what had happened they were shocked. All of them were determined to get this grime-grazer and sort him out. (But they were all so sweet natured that they were a bit sketchy about what sorting him out actually consisted of!)

The grime-grazer didn't think so. He thought they were a daft bunch of scaredy-cats and that they would probably have difficulty catching a cold, let alone catching him! He almost laughed out aloud at the bird's tearful story of her loss.

He grinned at the owls fearful voice. He was positively rejoicing when he left the hall at the end. He decided to head for the woods again. Things to do, people to see and PLACES TO GO!

Just then, Flame started to sing his haunting melody. People gathered round to watch Flame's eyes. There were many "Oohs" and "aahhs" as they watched the grime-grazer for the first time.

They saw him running through the trees, his long brown coat catching on twigs and bushes.

“I recognise that coat,” said Farmer Jon, stroking his silver beard thoughtfully.... “And that hat,” he added as the hat caught on an overhead branch and stayed suspended while the blue-grey man continued running on his purposeful journey.

Flames eyes flickered, as if somebody had changed channel, the they were all watching Lily and Ted watering the flower beds and laughingly throwing water over each other. As they watched, they saw Alice wandering around with a tray, nodding a lot. Next they saw Mrs Batty pegging out some washing. It was sunny!

The vision faded and there was silence in the hall as realisation dawned that the grime-grazer had been amidst them. He had heard the very thing that he mustn't hear and now they were all definitely doomed.

They looked at each other in disbelief. The silence went on and on....

The most beautiful singing filled the air. The acoustics of the high ceilinged building were exceptional and Flame's voice echoed around. The feeling of peace and serenity grew as they were enveloped in melody. It overtook the fretful feelings and left calm. When everybody left the hall, they were dignified but determined to find a way forward. It was still raining.

……Once the grime-grazer was in the centre of the woodland, he took out his magazine article. It was all about fashion and there were both male and female models showing off the winter lines. He didn't realise the article was from 1974. He thought this was THE look. He imagined himself dressed as they were. Wouldn't that be cool! Flared jeans and multi coloured scarves, pointy collars, floppy hats and large flowers on everything. Best of all, there in the background, sitting on a wall was a little green figure. She looked really cute. He wanted to visit The World.

He growled out aloud. "Grrrowl growwlllodd"

"Groowwwl Growwwlodd."

"Ggrroowwwwlodd."

But nothing happened. He didn't budge an inch. He was angry but he couldn't say it correctly. He tried again and again but to no avail. He smashed up a newly made nest instead, but it didn't make him feel any better.

……Walking home, Peanut asked Bean if he would please accompany her to the widow's house to see if she could convince her friends to come home. Boris was walking slightly ahead and was most interested to spot a copy of Zap the Wizard laying in a puddle. It had been bitten!

"Oh no," he exclaimed. "Look at this. This is the work of that grime-grazer. They eat the book rather than read it, to ingest the story. We underestimated this creature. He will know all sorts of things now. If nothing else he will easily be able to find his way around Odd. We thought he was still learning. Oh bother!"

"That's it, I have had enough, he added in an agitated voice. He stopped in his tracks. "That's odd, that's odd, that's odd," he called to the air. Nothing happened. "Would you believe it, that crafty grime-grazer has reversed the rules for everybody except ME! He obviously believed I would be a decent adversary or he wouldn't have bothered." Boris looked really cross, then quite sad. "You see? I really am of no use to you," he sighed.

"This is very bad. By eating this particular book, he is undoing the good that you both managed last year. He will be stopping the children from reaching us and he has effectively stopped me from reaching them." Boris paced up and down in agitation.

"Boris, Bean and I want to go to The World. We will bring everybody back, you'll see." Peanut told him. She didn't want to worry or upset him and he already looked pretty fed up. She knew they had to do this one thing. Boris shook his head. He didn't want to risk children. He felt there must be somebody else.

Peanut was quite insistent. She knew they could do this, and they were no more at risk than anybody else. "I don't want children to suffer." she pleaded. "I need to start doing something Boris."

"If we can get our friends back safely, stop the grime-grazer from even getting there and replenish the Zap book stocks then we will be able to concentrate on doing more good instead of forever trying to undo the bad that HE has made." she explained.

"Yes Boris," Bean added, "It makes perfect sense. Gathering up our folk has to be the start of our journey. Please ask everybody to watch the grime-grazer so we know where he is, just in case. Try to think of a remedy while we are away so that by the time we return we can deal with him swiftly."

"If nothing else, we can use that last wish to at least keep him in Odd where we know he will expire eventually and give us some respite," Peanut offered.

"That's a good idea," nodded Boris. "But do please be careful, I don't want to lose you. I wish there were more I could do to help." He sighed in frustration.

"Really Boris, it is not as though this is dangerous. We know what to do and we will not be long you'll see." Peanut could see that Boris wasn't going to argue, so she started to concentrate on the task ahead.

Boris had actually seen that Peanut wasn't about to give in, so he didn't bother to argue!

......Sandra had been feeling bored. She was always just 'good old Sandra'. She had never had a boyfriend, never been anywhere or done anything other than just being jolly old dependable Sandra, and quite frankly she was sick of it! The meeting had given her a great idea. She had missed her early years travel slot due to caring for others and that had been an end to it, or so she thought until the meeting. Today, she had learned how easy it would be to simply disappear and she was going to do it!

She headed home to collect a few things she thought a traveller might need. On the way through the wood, she talked aloud of all the things she would like to do. The grime-grazer listened with great interest.

"I will need a bag of food, a photograph of all my friends and family and some things to sell if I need any money. A hot water bottle and a flask would be good too... and a kettle." she ran through her rather strange list.

The grime-grazer started to feel very excited indeed. He couldn't get to The World because he couldn't pronounce the correct words - but he knew a lady who could! All he had to do was climb into her pocket when she wasn't looking. That should be easy, she was such a daydreamer she wasn't even looking where she was going now. He felt certain that Sandra would make an excellent vehicle.

......Boris and the children had lunch at the cottage then, with strict instructions to stay together, they left a sad and gloomy Boris. It wasn't even Sadday! Peanut took Flame with her because she couldn't be parted from him.

Outside, they both repeated the words. "That's odd, that's odd, that's odd!" ZZooom, crunch! They landed in a heap by a signpost, just as Pa Baddle had described.

'I'm tempted to visit Fast Harling (heart), just to have a look," Bean grinned.

"Oh no you don't," peanut grinned grabbing his arm. "We are on a mission, remember?"

Bean shrugged, "Maybe some other time if the super-highways are opening up to us, we may all be able to visit whenever we want to."

"Can you imagine that though Bean?" asked Peanut. "Just think for a while what that would mean. At the moment, if everything is reversed, anybody from here can get to Odd. Can you think what it is going to be like once they realise it? What would you do if your folks turned up looking for you? Or your old headmaster? A neighbour, the school bully?" They walked swiftly along the road West of Harling. Bean could see she had a point. It would not be at all desirable.

They passed lots of things they had forgotten about during their year in Odd. Peanut wished they could get past the dreadful smell, but that was one thing that didn't seem to be getting far enough away to forget about! There were a lot of road signs. Odd didn't need all these signs because there weren't any cars! They simply had handcrafted directional signposts and they were quite pretty. Before they rounded the corner, she looked back and saw the 'Give Way' triangle. She pointed it out to Bean.

He laughed, "If they insist." He put one hand to his forehead and staggered around in mock misery, "Oh, oh I can't bear it, oh woe is me."

Peanut joined him and began staggering, "I need a doctor, oh how awful, how dreadful." After a couple of minutes of giving way, they continued on their way, still laughing.

"How far along here is it to the widows house Bean?" Peanut asked. "Have you noticed that the sun is shining? That is one of the things I loved about Odd, despite the way it has been raining recently, I still think of it as a sunny place. I think it's all the laughter."

They had to jump onto the verge as a car screeched toward them at about eighty mile an hour, narrowly avoiding them. "That is another thing I love about Odd. Can you smell that smell? Petrol fumes and manure, not to mention that really horrid smell of weed killer that hurts your throat. Yuk!"

"It isn't really petrol fumes that do all the damage though if you think about it," Bean mused drawing breath as they jogged along. He looked up. "One aeroplane uses more fuel than fifty cars." Peanut glanced at him in surprise.

"Then I am doubly glad that Odd doesn't have any." she nodded. "You sort of forget these things when you recall what it was like here. I tend to remember television or computers, or even fast food!"

"Me too," agreed Bean. "But strangely I don't miss them as I thought I would. I suppose its because the conversations are lively and varied. There is always something new to learn or devise. Lets hope we manage to stop the grime-grazer, or all that will end."

"Do you remember the grumpy people and schools and bullies? Can you recall the strange red tape rules that seemed to click in every time somebody looked like they may be about to enjoy themselves?" Peanut grinned. "By now they have probably got an Enjoying-Yourself-Tax."

Bean laughed. "Ah good, here we are." he said as he saw the brown sign. "The widows house." The children turned right into the shady tree-lined walkway.

"Look out!" Bean just managed to grab Peanut and pull her out of the path of an oncoming vehicle. The lunatic motor-home driver leaned out of the open window. "Use your eyes you stupid... Peanut? Bean?"

The engine stalled as Mrs Crimble suddenly realised who she had almost mown down. She looked more than a touch embarrassed when she also realised that she had become one of those awful people that Peanut had told her about in The World. One of the ones with 'no manners' and 'not enough time to care.' But she did care. She climbed out of the drivers seat. "That's it, I think its time to go home. Have you come to get me?" she asked them tiredly.

"Yes Mrs Crimble, I think that would be for the best, don't you?" Peanut asked in that calm patient voice that you use on people who are dangerously unpredictable. In this situation, it was the exact voice to get results. It is also the last voice you would usually use when you feel totally freaked out with terror. However, Peanut managed to smile encouragingly at the unrecognisable Mrs Crimble. She smiled back and complied without a murmur.

Bean walked on one side of her and peanut on the other, still carrying a quiet Flame. As they reached the huge oak tree, Peanut said, “Okay, here we go.” She lifted Mrs Crimble’s right arm to her forehead and whispered “Well I never!”

“Well I never?” Asked the incredulous Mrs Crimble, and instantly vanished.

Chapter Ten

Looking around them, Bean and Peanut spotted most of the rest of their people around the pool.

"Hello!" said a breathless Peanut and Bean.

"Hi!" replied a couple of disinterested voices. They were laying face down on sun loungers around the poolside in the afternoon sunshine. Apparently it was their day off and they couldn't be bothered to be polite.

"It's me, Peanut," she tried again.

"Oh hi Peanut," said an equally disinterested voice. It was Mrs Batty. "Wuff!" said a sleepy Boots.

"Wuff? Who are you trying to kid?" asked a horrified Bean.

Boots had the grace to look up and acknowledge the children. "Wuff!" he nodded.

"Oh no, not you too? Surely you can still talk?" Bean looked really worried and Peanut was mortified.

“This isn’t right. What is wrong with you all? This is totally weird. You all look really relaxed but you are acting like aliens. You are not relaxed at all, you are just about comatosed. Don’t you realise that you have lost your politeness, your interest? Not to mention that the art of being interesting appears to have gone with it.”

They nodded and waved her away, as though she were some pesky fly annoying them.

Peanut looked at Bean in despair. She had never seen her friends like this before. Bean shrugged. He didn’t know what to do. He was just about to re-attempt to attain their attention when he spotted Shep.

Shep had always been a very proud dog-sheep. He had the wooliest black and white fleece that could ever be sheared. It went with the waggiest tail and the silkiest long black and white ears to ever frame a sweet doggie face.

At least that is how Shep used to look, but apparently not today. Bean was shocked. Right down one side read the words ‘mob rule’, on the other side it said ‘anarchy’. The words had been sheared in, right to the skin. “Shep?” Bean whispered.

Shep raised his sleepy head. “Wuff, Baaaaaa!” he said lazily, then returned unseeing to his sunbathing.

"I give in, what do we do now Peanut?" Bean asked.
"We have got to get them home. Thank goodness we came when we did. Come on, Boris is waiting for us."

Just then Alice came tripping through the open doorway of the house, seemingly not a care in the world. "Drinks," she trilled.

Peanut was not impressed by this, but strangely, all the others seemed to come momentarily alive.

As quick as a flash, Peanut ran to greet Alice. She grabbed the tray from her outstretched hands and said "Alice, how wonderful to see you. Come on everybody, into the shade for your refreshments." Grabbing Alice by the arm she frog marched her over the field and toward the towering oak tree.

She looked around frantically trying to spot an older member of their people. Her eyes finally rested upon Old Eric.

"Eric, you have already had your drink." Peanut smiled at him convincingly. Eric instantly lifted his arm to his head and scratched it. He scrunched his face up in puzzlement, frowning as he tried to recall drinking it. "Well," he replied, "I never..." Whoosh, he was gone!

This started the rest off, one by one Mrs Bundy, Lily, Ted, Jay, Gus, Mrs Batty and Henry all said the trigger words and vanished. Soon only Peanut, Shep, Boots and Bean remained.

"Wuff," said Boots.

"Wuff," said Shep.

"Let's take one each," Bean said. Peanut grabbed Boots. "Well I never" she said, holding her right arm to her brow. They vanished.

Bean followed with Shep. There on the grass where the crowd had been standing, sat a full drinks tray. The birds sang on, in puzzlement.

Everybody was heartily welcomed home by all their friends and families. There was a lot of concern at the state of them all. Each person was gently led away for some peace and rest.

......Once Sandra was ready, she went to her front garden and took a look around to see if anybody was looking. She had left a note on the kitchen table explaining where she had gone. She left another on the mantle piece above her kitchen stove and another under the stone on the front porch. This yucky rain was really getting to her.

The grime-grazer watched Sandra as she looked skyward and said,

“That’s odd”, in a nice clear voice. “That’s odd”... The grime-grazer made his move. He ran full pelt toward Sandra, he could see an ideally situated pocket as he approached. He took a flying leap off the end of the garden wall toward it... “That’s odd.” Sandra completed. As she vanished the grime-grazer hit her pocket, he grabbed it just as he was ricocheted off at right angles, like a bouncy ball. He landed painfully in a clump of nettles.

“Ow, grooowl, oouch growl!” he climbed out and looked around for Sandra but she was gone. He was so angry, though nobody would have noticed any difference in him. He was also very sore and very tingly.

Sandra didn’t know what she really needed to take on her travels. The final item she had picked up and stuffed into her bulging pockets had been a blue bouncy ball that she liked to play with in times of stress. It had unwittingly saved her from an unwanted stowaway.

......Boris was very pleased at the safe return of his children, as he considered both Peanut and Bean to be. “While you were gone, the birds have been trying to keep an eye on the grime-grazer. We have managed to fence off an inner part of the forest in the hope of keeping the little blighter contained.”

“He sleeps quite a lot. We know because the sun comes out. The rest of the time he seems to be practising his words of escape, so I am told. He is really trying hard to get to The World. The pigeons tell me that it will be a while before he manages it because he is much too growly, but I wouldn't be too sure. He is sure to find a way around it."

"Well we did," replied Peanut. "We had to," she explained. "Boots and Shep are unable to talk and we needed to find a way to bring them home, so we took one each and just did as the others had done. That worked."

They all stood together in the late afternoon drizzle and stared through the grey mistiness into the forest, like it could provide the answers they needed to put their Odd to rights.

"Come on, lets get you warm and dry," Boris said eventually. "You can have some dinner. I have a lovely beef casserole with dumplings simmering back at the cottage. You are hungry?" he asked.

They were indeed! The conversation at the table was avid as they described their afternoon and the events of Odd in their short absence. Boris hadn't thought of any plan but he had stumbled upon a further problem. "Even if we do capture the grime-grazer, what do we do with him?" he asked.

Nobody had thought of that. Peanut closed her eyes and tried to visualise the grime-grazer. Flame remained peaceful, as he had for the entire day. Even in The World, he had looked all around him and taken it all in, but been silent. The plume remained lowered.

The sun tried to manage a final weak glimmer that evening as it set in the west. "Something tells me that the grime-grazer is asleep." Boris noted.

"Do you think he is storing up his energy or is this normal?" Peanut asked Boris.

"Your guess is as good as mine little one. I wouldn't trust him though. It seems to me that just as we have this evil creature worked out, he seems to be aware of it and changes tack."

......The grime-grazer was indeed asleep, stung all over, his fur tingled and his skin hurt. It felt as though it were on fire! His pride was also slightly wounded. He was just glad that nobody had seen his foiled attempt at travel. Licking his sore arms and hands he had finally curled up, sulking on his stack of leaves and fallen asleep.

......When Sandra arrived at the signpost offering Fast Harling (heart) or Garbledshams - (reading had never been a strong point), she sat a while and watched a tractor. It was making loud chugging noises and sticking out of a hole at the most peculiar angle. The thought occurred to Sandra that the tractor could get stuck if it continued. (Thought was another thing that wasn't a strong point with Sandra!)

The driver who had been tipped upside down in the cab for about two hours also guessed he might be stuck.

Sandra decided to go and see the widow's house where people carried their rooms around like human snails. This place sounded really neat to Sandra and she wanted to see it all for herself. She passed the "Give Way 100 yards" sign and the pile of horse manure.

As she strolled along she was reading all the discarded packets and wrappers like they were clues on a treasure trail. It was all terribly exciting - but then she was a bit strange!

When she got to the cottage, Sandra clapped her hands together in pure delight. She was so excited. Once she had seen the huge oak tree from where she knew she could go home if she chose, she went to look around the field at all the rooms. Nobody had told her that they *belonged* to people.

She poked her head inside this one and that one. Jumping up and down so she could see into the windows of the taller motorised ones and crawling down on her hands and knees to inspect the coloured triangular ones that folk around here seemed to refer to as 'tense'. They didn't look tense to her. The looked quite relaxed and a little bit funky actually, she considered.

After walking around the field, Sandra climbed into the cab of her favourite snail home. This couldn't be any more difficult to use than a ride-on lawnmower she decided. With a foot on the pedal she whacked it into gear and shot forward through the hedge and into the next field. After a few attempts at this, covering no less than two fields and four hedges, she began to get the hang of it.

......The crazy motorist, minus his mobile phone which he couldn't find anywhere, had finally managed to get his car back on the road. It was limping along the Chase road, bumper trailing along the surface with the most awful scratchy sound, front grill all bent in, but moving at least. The front number plate was missing and the driver was not in a very happy mood. That was when he first met Sandra.

......Sandra was feeling really pleased. She knew she could manage to drive one of these things. It was easy. Foot down to the floor she lurched through the fifth hedge and straight into the side of a battered car. For a little while she sat there, quite dazed. The other motorist began to believe that actually this day wasn't happening at all. He was simply caught in an ironic nightmare.

"How do you do?" Sandra offered her gloved hand through the missing window to the seated male driver.

"Charmed I'm sure," sneered the sarcastic voice.

He shook her hand and Sandra's knees turned to jelly. She

turned bright red and giggled, Well, I must be going. she simpered. Climbing back into the stolen motor home, she lurched a few more times and was gone.

The crazy motorist gave up and just sat there, where he had been shunted into the verge. He guessed that today wasn't his day.

Chapter Eleven

......Mrs Bundy was sitting in her big comfy armchair in her own kitchen. Mr Bundy had made her a cup of tea but the cup remained untouched beside her. Mr Bundy took her hand gently. "It is so good to have you home my dear. Won't you drink a little of the lovely refreshing tea I made for you?" he coaxed.

Mrs Bundy pulled her little green scarf more tightly around her, stroking the end of it. She seemed totally dazed.

"You poor sweet lady," Mr Bundy tried again. "You are all in, perhaps a little something to eat? Would it make you feel better? What can I tempt you with?" he tried again.

Still no response. Mr Bundy stopped trying and lit the kitchen fire. "A little warmth won't go amiss, I'm sure." He spoke gently while keeping an eye on his poor tired wife.

Mrs Bundy looked around her for the first time, but stayed very still. She watched her husband as he lit the fire and built it up with logs and paper bricks. When he stood up, he checked her cup again. "This is cold now my dear. I'll make you another.

Here, let me hang your scarf up for you, or you won't feel the benefit when you go out." He put out his hand to take it.

Suddenly, the scarf moved all of its own accord. It stood up snarling and hissing. Mr Bundy jumped back terrified, but he was too late. The thing had sunk its very sharp white teeth into his finger.

Mr Bundy screamed. The green thing screamed. Mr Bundy shook his hand back and forth, jolting the nasty spitting screaming green thing up and down but it had a serious hold on him. Blood dripped onto the kitchen floor.

Finally, while Mr Bundy fought for his life, Mrs Bundy seemed to snap out of her trance like state. She jumped up horrified at the scene in front of her and grabbed the nearest saucepan from the stove. BANG! She brought it crashing down on the green creature. It dropped like a stone, limp and lifeless to the floor.

Mr Bundy's heart was jumping so fiercely in his chest he thought it was going to bounce right out. He ran to the sink and put his hand in cold water. The water turned first pink, then red with blood. He wrapped a clean cloth around the bite mark and looked for some antiseptic cream to keep the wound clean.

Once his hand was sorted out, he went to the lifeless green creature still lying on the kitchen floor. He stooped down. After wrapping the thing tightly in a towel, he put it in a biscuit tin and tied down the lid, to take it to Boris. He had a pretty good idea of what this creature was.

Peanut and Bean had been drinking their hot chocolate when Flame burst into agitated song. His plume was bolt upright, his wings flapped and his eyes clouded over. Boris, Bean and Peanut all stared into Flame's eyes. There was no mistaking the scene unfurling before their very eyes. They saw Mr and Mrs Bundy fighting the green creature.

"A FEMALE GRIME-GRAZER! Here in Odd. Grief!" they cried in unison. Leaping to their feet but unsure of what to do next, they stood transfixed. Their hearts were thumping as they saw what was happening. When Mrs Bundy smashed the nasty creature with a saucepan you should have heard them all shouting their encouragement.

When Flames eyes went back to normal, they all sighed a deep sigh of relief and sat back down. "I feel quite shaky," Peanut said.

"Oh my goodness," Boris eventually said. "Do you know what this means? How very stupid of me, they can come here! He doesn't need to go there, don't you see?" He looked at the children as realisation finally dawned on them too.

"That was one heck of a fight though," Bean said in awe.

"That's the thing about them though," sighed Boris. They infiltrate your way of living and eventually you have to become like them to fight them. That is not how it should be. Who wants to live like that anyway?"

"Do they ever get tired of it Boris?" Bean asked. "It stands to reason that they must want something more too doesn't it? Eventually?"

"No son. I think you are right in one way, but not with these things. People tend to fight when they are threatened. I cannot imagine somebody wanting to fight all the time but these creatures, well, they seem to be programmed wrong somehow. They enjoy it! They love the destruction as much as I love peace. The gentlefolk around here certainly are not up to this. They are sweet and kind, nor should they have to learn how to fight. This has to stop." He stood up and paced the floor.

The children sipped the rest of their hot chocolate and watched Boris.

"Boris," Peanut said quietly. "I think I have an idea. Does anybody around here play football?"

"Yes, all the time. Why do you ask?"

"I need to borrow some equipment. I think I will need your help." Peanut continued to mull the idea over thoughtfully.

Just then, there was a knock at the door. Bean opened it to see

Mr and Mrs Bundy standing there, shivering. Mr Bundy was clutching a biscuit tin tied with string.

"Hello, come on in, come on, up to the fire. Give me your coats." He took the tin from Mr Bundy's hands. Both the Bundys were white with shock. Peanut ran to get them some hot sweet tea as they settled themselves.

"We thought that you would want that," Mr Bundy nodded toward the tin. He shivered despite being right next to the fire and played with the bandage on his hand in a distracted manner.

"Well my dears, you are just in time," Boris told them. "Our Peanut here has a plan," he said with some delight. "She says she needs to borrow some sports equipment." Boris turned to Peanut. Our Mr Bundy here is in charge of the sports facilities at the hall," he explained. "He has the kcy to all the equipment."

Peanut handed them both their cups of tea. She felt it would be the best thing for shock. "The last thing you should be doing after having such a start is wandering around in the cold, you know that surely?"

Mr Bundy nodded. "We are both very unsettled. At least the walk made us feel a little less useless."
"Oh come on, you are hardly useless. You must have wrestled

that creature like a professional. I almost felt sorry for it at one point," Boris joked.

"Well it didn't feel very professional at the time. I was frightened. The rest was instinct. Now young lady," Mr Bundy turned toward Peanut. "What particular sports stuff do you need and when will you need it?" he asked.

"I could do with eight footballs of different colours if possible and two portable goal posts. The ones with nets already in would be good, do you have any?"

"Yes, four different colours plus white and black ones and we have the nets too."

"What colours have you got?" Peanut was feeling really sleepy. It had been a long day and all she wanted to do was rest. The lack of sunlight made her more sleepy than usual.

"Red, blue, yellow and green."

"Brilliant! I need only one of the red, two blue and two yellow. The rest can be black and white, we can leave the green, they would only get lost in the grass anyway. Could we rustle up some players too, eight children would be ideal. They need to be of the sensible variety though, and able to follow instructions to the letter."

Boris nodded and made a note on his pad. "Bean, can you get

some sensible players together lad?"

"Also Boris, please could you be referee and Mr Bundy, would you mind being on stand-by with that wish?"

"Of course we can," agreed Boris and Mr Bundy in unison, looking pleased to be involved.

"Oh, and we will need a whistle."

"I will get everything first thing tomorrow," Mr Bundy agreed.

Bean looked really intrigued. "What's the plan Peanut?"

"We are going to play football," smiled Peanut happily, like butter wouldn't melt! "It will accidentally be near the grime-grazer. I can get a check on where he is from Flame, in the morning. The grime-grazer must not suspect a thing. To him it must look as though we haven't a clue that he is there, we will simply be playing a nice little practice game. That way we should stay safe. When I say the word we must go home and leave some of the sports stuff behind."

"Ahh," Bean nodded. He thought that Peanut intended to capture the grime-grazer in a football net. He guessed that the wish would help them somehow but it still seemed a bit of a long shot to him.

"Now, I am off to bed," yawned a tired Peanut. Everybody agreed.

Chapter Twelve

The next day dawned grey and drizzly. When Peanut got to the kitchen she found everybody already eating breakfast. She took a slice of toast and grinned at them all, feeling curiously light-hearted for the first time in ages. "Is everybody ready to go and catch a grime-grazer?" she asked.

"I have been thinking about that," Bean said. "What if the grime-grazer doesn't want to be caught? I mean, he is not likely to be stupid enough to walk into our nets."

"I already thought of that," Peanut smiled and nodded. "I am guessing he won't actually mind being caught, it is when he realises that he can't escape that we will have some trouble I suspect. We must be careful to use the wish if one of us is in danger. While he doesn't know we are there to get him, we are safe. Aren't we Boris?" Peanut looked momentarily worried.

"We can but try," agreed Boris, glad that he could at least be there this time.

Mrs Bundy volunteered to clear away the breakfast things, providing that the green thing in the biscuit tin was first locked away in a metal trunk. "I don't want to be left alone with that thing," she fretted.

Boris did just that and showed Mrs Bundy so she felt reassured. Then after she had kissed them all and wished them luck, they set off toward the meeting hall.

"Poppy would like to play football I am sure. I will run and get her," Bean offered. He was a swift runner and even with the detour he would be with them again in no time.

The others carried on. They hadn't been walking very long when they met Gus, Harry and Steven. The boys agreed to play football without hesitation. They loved the idea!

At the cart stop a cart stopped! So they rode the rest of the way. The pony was called Sunshine. She was a beautiful grey and very happy in her work. She said she would wait for them to gather the equipment to take into the forest. This was going better than Peanut had hoped.

The boys were soon joined by Poppy and Bean, who was looking a little warm and sounding out of breath. To be fair, they had run all the way.

Peanut looked around her. She checked Flame's eyes the second his comb stood up. There in the wood was their target. He was knocking out cobwebs with a stick, he looked tired though.

Peanut saw the little brook and a diamond shaped boulder. She knew where that was!

She took the opportunity to tell everybody what they were to do when they got there. It was imperative that they get this right first time, there may never be a second chance.

"Bean, who else do you know that can join us, we are four players short?" Peanut asked as they travelled toward the forest.

"Jay and Alice, that's two. Errrr, I know, Henry and Aggie? They live near here, we can call in on them and see if they are free," Bean said.

So it was that the cart stopped at the two houses along the way. Soon enough they were all briefed and ready to go. They had the strict instructions not to say the words 'grime-grazer' any more.

Peanut glanced a Flame again. She saw the vision of the nasty grime-grazer climbing into a hollow of the elm tree. He turned around a few times, sniffed the air and then curled up to go to sleep.

"Ugh!" Poppy shivered. "He looks so small, you would never know what an evil piece of work he is just by looking at him."
"I would," Peanut assured her. "I watched him eating a sparrow today. It wasn't pleasant. I felt quite sick when he was finished," she grimaced.

"Okay, shush, we are almost there. Now remember, a short game, no names mentioned and then we pack up almost everything and leave, got it?" She put Flame down as they rounded the last corner and asked him to please be quiet. Flame didn't like being left but he did as his 'mum' asked him.

Boris and Mr Bundy set up the goal posts. Chatting in what they hoped was a nonchalant manner. Nobody dared to look at the tree where they all knew the grime-grazer lay, just in case he had already woken. Not one of them wanted to be the person to mess it all up.

They tried to concentrate on looking carefree and cheery. First they all practised ball control and goal shots, making as much noise as possible to alert their prey. Next they started to play. Soon a pretty good game was in progress. Poppy and Henry were in goal, Boris blew the whistle for an off-side, and again when a goal was scored, which was pretty often, so they could cheer a lot. With all the adrenaline flowing the attack was much better than the defence.

Finally, at five goals to three, Boris called time. Everybody was soaked through. They laughed and chatted and hoped to fury that they sounded just how they usually did.

Picking up the practice balls (except one), Peanut put them into a net and said, “Come on everybody, lets go and get a drink. We can come back and get the nets when we have to gather firewood after lunch.” I could do with at least an hours rest, I am completely worn out,” she called loudly.

They all climbed back into the cart with the net and set off for home. The cart trundled slowly up the hill. Putting her finger to her lips, Peanut waved to her friends and jumped out, rolling slightly into the verge.

Bean followed suit, though he still wasn’t sure what he had to do yet. Boris and Mr Bundy joined them. But they rolled quite a lot more than the children did, because of their old bones and the damp weather.

Crouching low, the four of them returned to the clearing and waited out of sight. Suddenly, there was a rustling noise. It was a lot closer that Peanut had expected and she almost jumped out of her skin. Then she realised it was only Flame.

She felt worried that he wouldn’t manage to remain silent. She put her finger to her lips to remind him, but he knew. All he did was to stand in front of her, then his eyes clouded over and she could see the grime-grazer. Flame was helping her!

Peanut watched. The grime-grazer was biting a goal net. This was as she had suspected. Initially, his only interest, having been rudely awakened from his nap, would be to cause as much damage as he could. Peanut had ensured that she let him know just how long he had to make his trouble. Or maybe he was worried about the nets, despite their large holes, maybe he wanted to be sure that he couldn't get caught up in them. Or perhaps he was hungry!

The grime-grazer laughed with glee when he realised just how big a hole he had managed to make. He looked up and saw the other goal post. He walked towards it. Peanut could now see him clearly so Flame stood aside. She held her breath. "Oh, no!" she thought, "he's missed it."

The grime-grazer walked straight past the semi-concealed football. "Oh, its too well hidden, he isn't going to see it." She felt annoyed. "Turn around," she silently willed.

Just as she had given up hope, he turned back toward the long grass and stopped in his tracks. Looking furtively around, he took a step toward the ball. Then another, then he almost ran to it. He reached out a hairy blue-grey hand and touched the smooth shiny surface. He stroked it.

Peanut didn't dare hope.

The grime-grazer walked around the football, as though assessing it for something. It was only a little taller than he was. He crouched down, then as though finding what he was looking for, he reached out again. Finally, he sat down, right next to the ball. This was excruciating. Peanut had to breathe. She did so as quietly as possible, not daring to move a muscle. Bean, Boris, Flame and Mr Bundy watched too. They just thought the grime-grazer was looking to see if he could let the air out, or eat it. Only Peanut knew what she was hoping against hopes would happen. Her fingers dug around in her pocket as she watched, to check she still had the eraser from the top of her pencil. Yes, there it was!

Then it happened. The grime-grazer went all long and skinny and wriggled and slithered into the bright red shiny football through the air hole. Peanut jumped up so fast that she almost toppled straight back down again. She pushed Flame into Bean's hands and ran the swiftest she had ever run in her life, toward the football.

As she neared, she saw the blue-grey feet pull into the ball. The grime-grazer was struggling to turn around. He could hear the sound of heavy fast-approaching footsteps. With a superb rugby style dive, Peanut grabbed the ball and pushed the pencil eraser into the air hole, effectively bunging the gap to stop the Grime-grazer's escape.

As she stood up she spun the ball triumphantly above her head like a trophy. The biggest smile covered her freckly face. She positively beamed. The sun had come out.

It was only when Peanut was running full pelt toward the ball that Boris realised what this brave little lady had concocted. He had told her to outwit the creature and outwit him she had! "I am so proud of you little one." he hugged her.

Bean and Mr Bundy weren't far behind him. "Wow Peanut, that was brilliant," Bean congratulated her. "I would never have thought of that in a million years!"

Peanut looked embarrassed. "I couldn't have done it without you all and I am not going to take all the credit either," she warned them fiercely.

Bean handed Flame over to her. Flame looked adoringly into her eyes. "You won't need the Birthday wish Peanut," he said in a smooth dreamy soft voice. Peanut was startled. "Oh yes, you can talk," she reminded herself out loud.

"Boris, you can do the honours," Flame suggested, nodding toward the ball.

"Yes of course, my magic works again doesn't it?" Boris agreed. He raised his arms and his cloak swept back. "With all the magic in this land I command you grime-grazer to stay forever in your

bright red shiny football egg. May you rest in peace and may your evil fade and die."
The football, which had been jumping and jolting around while the furious, snarling, spitting, evil grime-grazer fought to get out, was immediately still. It was the end. He was caught.

Boris was taking no chances. He carried the ball in front of him where he could keep his eyes on it as they returned jubilantly to the waiting Mrs Bundy.

Chapter Thirteen

Despite it only being Theirday, the people flocked to the wizards cottage to congratulate them all. The news had spread like wildfire and everybody wanted to hear how it had been achieved.

"Boris, can you please use your magic to replenish the stocks of 'Zap the Wizard?'" the children requested. "Then our work will truly be complete."

Boris concentrated and carried out a Book Replenishing Spell so that children in The World could come to them if they needed to.

"He really is quite good isn't he?" Peanut teased as he finished.

Poppy nodded. "It's a bit like being inside a television, living here. Things that I used to only dream of actually happen here in Odd. That's the way it is, and that's the way I like it!"

Bean came over to speak to Peanut. "How did you know your plan would work?" he asked her puzzled.

"I didn't," she replied. "I just hoped with all my heart that it would. I figured that the grime-grazer would never previously have seen a Red Backed Buckle Bum's egg before. He was relying on his instinct. I bet he had no idea that he was supposed to dissolve into an egg. He was probably just as in the dark as we were. I suspect that he couldn't believe his luck when he found a hole to get through!"

She laughed. "I still can't believe its over. I am so very happy." Peanut grinned, hugging her arms around her. She stood there smiling like an idiot, soaked to the skin, hair all bedraggled and looking as though she had been through a hedge backward - which she just about had.

Flame took a moment to himself. Standing in the doorway he looked out upon the restored land of Odd. He felt proud to be Oddish. Laughter rang out all around him and he knew he was amidst good friends. This is the way it should be. In his happiness and purely because he could, he created a huge rainbow right across the grey skies.

Peanut went and stood alongside him. She smiled. "That is beautiful Flame," she said, looking up at the sky. "A very clever way of drawing a line or two under our terrible week and marking the start of our happier times to come."

Flame looked pleased. "Life is good." he stated simply. Looking down he noticed a dead butterfly. He frowned. Stooping down, he scooped up the bright creature in his wings and put the lifeless insect to his lips.

"Oh Flame, kissing him won't help. He is dead," she added as gently as she could. "They don't live very long," she added by way of an explanation.

But Flame simply breathed into the butterflies mouth... The wings started to flutter, slowly at first, then faster.

"Grief!" exclaimed Peanut. "I could have sworn it was dead."

Boris joined them. "It was dead Peanut, didn't I tell you? Flame is quite magical, he is a giver of life, hope and dreams. Odd is truly blessed!"

Flame sang his sweet song and all the birds flocked around the garden to join in the chorus.

Mrs Bundy was making sandwiches for everybody as fast as she could. Boots and Shep had found their voices at last and were making up for lost time by talking even more than Mrs Batty - which is saying something!

Mrs Crimble muscled her way into the crowded kitchen and began making tea, coffee and hot chocolate for all she was worth.

Boris stood back a little in the sunshine, looking in through the open doorway. The happy sounds and smells of good food reached him as he contemplated his world and counted his blessings. "I could magic the food and drink," he thought amused. "But that would spoil their fun!" It had only been a week ago that their entire way of life was turned on its head. It wouldn't be long before Flame could fly. He would probably look fantastic with all his bright feathers fanned out around him.

Peanut was still chatting with Bean and Poppy when Steven handed her a note. She unfolded it and began to read. "Oh Pants!" she said. The others stared at her. "It's Sandra. You will never guess, she has left!" she exclaimed, eyes wide with amazement. "She says she has gone to The World to travel. What do you think will happen now? We have reversed everything, how will she ever get back?"

Bean looked up at the ceiling. "I think she will get homesick. She has never travelled before. It won't be like she thinks it will be. By the time she is ready to come home we will have worked out how to get her home, I'm sure. She may even enjoy it."

Pa Baddle had been sitting quietly in the corner of the kitchen, sipping a cup of sweet tea and watching the children play. Suddenly a weird noise made him jolt the tea skywards. It came down and scalded his legs. "Aaarrrggh!" he shouted.

The noise continued, 'Buuuuzzzz abuzz a buzz buzz buzzza, buzza, buzza.' Pa Baddle's eyes widened with shock as he looked around the kitchen, still frantically brushing at his scalded trouser legs with his handkerchief.

Boris ran in, looking around. “Its coming from your pocket,” he said, pointing a wavering index finger towards the over coat. Pa stood up and gingerly pulled the pocket open with finger and thumb so he could see in it.

“It’s that thing!” Boris pointed toward the silver box he had picked up in The World.

Pa Baddle pulled the box out; ‘Buzz a buzz a zub zub zub, buzzza buzza buz’ continued the noise Pa opened the box to look inside and there, staring back at him was an abseiling bumblebee!

Everybody crowded around to see it. It seemed to be contained in a screen and there were lots of numbers below it. None of them knew they were looking at a mobile phone. Their expressions ranged from mildly amused to freaked out bewildered. “Grief! That’s odd!” Peanut said, then clasped a hand over her mouth.

“Ahh, you think so do you? Then just you come over here a minute.” Boris waved his hand over toward the kitchen window.

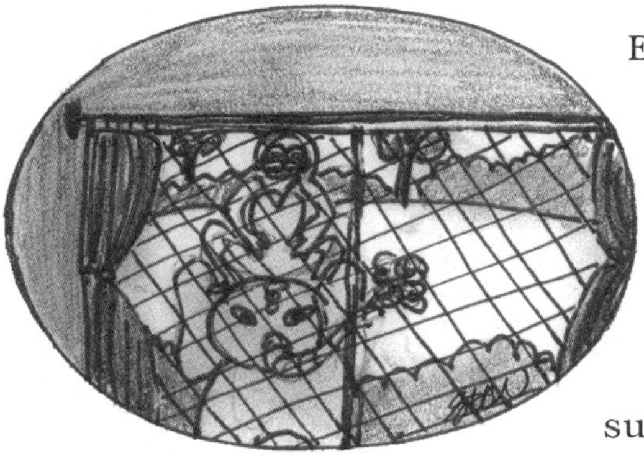

En-mass, the group crossed the room to look out and see what Boris was looking at.

Outside, in the front garden they saw a toad wearing sunglasses, riding around on the back of an elephant. The elephant was skipping in happiness with a bunch of meadow daisies clutched tightly in his trunk.

"Now *that* is REALLY ODD!" he said and they all laughed.

The End.

The prices shown below were correct at the time of going to press. However, Barkers Publishing reserve the right to show new retail prices on covers which may differ from those previously advertised in the text or elsewhere.

You can order copies of *Zap the Wizard and the Land of Odd*, or the sequel '*Really Odd*' by completing the form below or visit the web site at www.myspace.com/gillypurrfect.

Please supply ....copies of *Zap the Wizard and the Land of Odd*, at £3.99 per book (plus postage and packing).

Please supply .... copies of *Really Odd*, at £4.99 per book (plus postage and packing).

I enclose my cheque/ postal order made payable to G. Wilkinson. Send to:
G Wilkinson, PO Box 1218, NORWICH, NR16 2WS.

Postage and Packing:

UK and BFPO customers please send a cheque or postal order (no currency) and allow one pound for postage and packing for the first book plus 50p for each additional book.

Overseas customers, including Eire, please allow two pounds for postage and packing for the first book plus one pound for each additional book ordered.

Please complete in BLOCK CAPITALS

NAME ....

ADDRESS ....

....

....

....POSTCODE ....

I have enclosed cheque/postal order number ....for the

amount of £ .... sterling.

Alternatively, for credit card sales, please visit www.bluemoonshop.info, and remember to allow the cost of P & P as above.